also by brook blander

now that I'm here; lyrics from the mud to the sun
Personal: Intimate Comforts of Reflection
Lyrics of an Awakening
Soul Spoken
From This Day Forward

BROOK BLANDER

a historical fiction novel

The Kijani River Series

ebonyLotus | Publishing

Published by ebonyLotus | Publishing
12650 North Beach Street, Suite #114-55, Fort Worth, TX 76244
(800) 356-5023
www.ebonylotus.com

Paperback Library of Congress Control Number: TXu 1-845-801

Paperback ISBN: 978-0-9832988-0-9

For more books by Brook Blander, visit www.brookblander.com

Cover Photo Location Credits:
      Laura Plantation, Vacherie, Louisiana
      Ashtabula Plantations, Pendleton, South Carolina

Author Photo Credit: Dream Image Photography, Greenville, SC *to my ancestors, for my ancestors*

...especially my guiding angel, Juanita...

...for being a black sheep in green pointed toe heels with me in our journey through this life and beyond.

mercy |ˈmərsē|
noun (pl. **mercies**)

• compassion or forgiveness shown toward someone whom it is within one's power to punish or harm
• an event to be grateful for, esp. because its occurrence prevents something unpleasant or provides relief from suffering
• (esp. of a journey or mission) performed out of a desire to relieve suffering; motivated by compassion

before

THERE WAS SOMETHING BEYOND COURAGE in them, something able to abandon fear and worry, and engage hefty ambitions. A piece of soap, two blankets for when the babies come, a clean dress, folded and rolled, a pair of pants and ripped pages from a Bible shoved deep down in a potato sack. Their minds were already there, rooted and growing hundreds of miles away in a place they never visited. The words on the letter read "...free and we are alive. Come." Not used to happiness in excessive amounts, they gorged on their fantasies to ease their growing hunger and null the pain of letting go of the ones to be left behind. They know their sorrowful faces will be the heaviest bundle to carry and the most difficult to unload. In their minds, they know they must leave before they are gone to prevent them from looking back through the darkness. They would have to be tough and swift when they barge into the night hungry as lions, for if any sinister predator of the night got hold of them, it would be death.

Or torture.

Or both.

It would be machetes and vicious dogs turned loose on men, women and children. Canine razor teeth would strip the flesh from the bones

---

until blood ran and soaked the ground. It would be strings of saliva dropping heavy with dangling meat of muscles formed by lifetimes of strenuous labor. Gaping cavities in arms, thighs and backs would reveal gnawed bones. Effusive laughter from the mouths of patrolmen amid the tormenting screams and cries would croon into the darkness. Vainglorious patrolmen would bring word and the remains in broad daylight. They would stand upon wide porches of masters for rewards of coins, a cool drink and a swift pat of their backs. All the while, mangled body parts would bake under the sun on the backs of wagons, open and exposed for all to see. A swarm of flies would indulge in the immoderate meal and mangy dogs would sink their dirty teeth into pieces of meat and run dragging the limb or intestine or torso. Oh, how the masters would be proud and the other Whites would be pleased.

Then those left behind, would dare to question God of his decision to choose the varmint over the lives of those they love, for it was they who prayed without ceasing, who clutched their faith and stuffed it in every open space of their beings. It was they who believed wholeheartedly and in their own way. Who called on His favor by performing at their best. In the extra attention they gave to wiping the molasses jar clean of the sticky syrup and gentle cuts to skin the dead deer. In the way they gave added pats to the soil around the crops, the way they picked fruit from the trees with tender tugs, and they did not complain about the hot sun. It was they who believed they transacted with Him when they dropped their eyes to give the Whites what they wanted in exchange for the lives of their loved ones on the run – and to hide their terror and to hide their joy.

chapter 1

WHAT WAS LEFT OF THE SUN crouched behind towering trees and branches laden with Spanish moss.

"They gon' make it. I'm sure they gon' make it. Right, Sylvia? They gon' get there just fine. Right?"

"They will. You just keep praying for their protection. Everything gon' be alright. God gon' cover them out of here. You just got to believe it." Sylvia believed it for her heavy-hearted friend, Lu. She had to believe it. It was the greater side of what could happen.

Lu's cabin was filled tight with women. The plantation had a quiet rumble in the cabin just off the main path where the women were moving and frying dough to pack for the ones fleeing when the orange sun faded from the sky. They hummed deep and low from far within their bosoms. In the kitchen, they busied themselves with their tasks and did not look at each other except to ask for more lard or a piece of muslin to wrap the warm fried bread. Each had their own path to pave, they needed to find a place of rest to settle with their fright. Organized as they were, kneading dough, pulling dough, frying dough and sprinkling flour on the table amidst a fog of burning lard, in the silence of their beings, there was ransacking, tossing, turning, tussling, sadness, happiness and proper turmoil. They were wise and built themselves to sustain suffering and strife, but if their eyes touched, if they made sense of what they were doing they would collapse into each other and fall to pieces. A cool breeze waved the curtain nailed into the clapboard above the window. Sylvia knew she was in the midst of something bigger and more powerful than mere packing and preparations. The waves in her stomach told her so. Or, maybe it was the glimpse of the stars through the open window as they took their place in a clear sky. They settled far apart from each other, yet near enough for their lights to work together, led by the glowing moon. They were one—the stars, the moon and the women— each doing their own work to create something greater than what they were alone.

Their hopes and dreams were packed inside rolled socks and mended into worn shirts. For two days, those fleeing delivered their belongings, piece by piece, to Lu's house for packing. It was a way to hide their intentions elsewhere and not in their own homes. The one in charge, the one insistent on being called First Lady, could havoc through their space at any time for any self-indulgent reason. She knew the young were too young to deny themselves what beckoned outside the town of Mercy and they knew her watchful eyes were on them. Sylvia placed a bit of herself in the pocket of an apron she folded and pressed down the half-filled potato sack. Not too full or the strain would cause them to tire and hunger before they should. She did not pack an entire Bible stuffed in a pair of rolled pants. Instead, she packed only pages to ease the weight. She ripped several soft, thin sheets of paper from Psalms and all from the book of Exodus because in there, they made it.

She could hear the gathering outside in the damp, dew-filled grass. Lu wiped a staggering tear with the back of her hand without pause to her busy work, tying the last pieces of warm bread in cloth.

"They gone be alright, I tell you," Sylvia consoled with a hand on Lu's shoulder. Her friend's hands trembled as she tied and retied the knot.

"He's the only boy I got left." Lu said.

"I know."

"Don't know why he can't be alright with being here. It's that wife of his wanna get up and go. He do any and everything she tell him and he don't give a fuss about it." She looked at Sylvia with tears sitting on the rim of her eyelids. "Don't make a lick of sense to me why he let her run over him like that. Man supposed to run his family, not the wife."

Sylvia had no word of comfort. She was enduring her own share of a man running his family. Rubbing her hand across Lu's back, her friend could no longer confine her tears.

"You go on and let it out now. They don't need to see you like this before they go into night. You gotta give 'em comfort. You just go'on and get it out." She wrapped her arms around Lu and rocked her. "Go on. You gotta be stronger in a little while 'cause you gotta give 'em everything you got and be left with a little bit of nothing." Sylvia could have cried without persuasion but instead tightened her throat and her heart the way she did when her own sons were taken from her. The lumbering despair in Lu's bawls shot through the cabin without prejudice. Soon they were all using the hem of aprons to wipe their eyes and hugs were extended to lend and borrow bearings. It was time, everything was ready. Women with babies on their hips or wrapped on their backs fast asleep stood with torn hope falling from their eyes as they kissed husbands and older children goodbye. New wives clung to the necks of their new husbands until their mothers pried them loose and placed them on their bosoms making them children again. The curtains continued to flap until they were out the windows flailing in the cool breeze, and the night they all prayed for strength to make it through, continued to come.

The Lions—as they were called, the brave souls in pursuit of their rightful freedom—wrestled with joy and sadness. Their faces smiled and frowned at the same time but the darkness was black and covered their indisposition. They did not hug with might or length for if they did, they would be softened and fright would creep in and cripple their bravery. The four-day journey to Hartha Gables called for their will more than anything and they kept it secured with a stoic conscience. Hartha Gables was a town only a few years old and it was the Promise Land on earth. There were no masters, no slaves and the ground was pure of gray memories and crimson bloodstains. The seventeen people and two babies in wombs were the first to leave in over three months. The last group did not make it and were found strewn on both plantations, disjointed and unidentifiable except for two bashed heads still attached to the arm-less torso.

"Won't see you no more on this side, but I'll be waiting for you when you reach Heaven." A grandmother said her peace with the fleeting wave of a stringy, veined hand to her two grands. Her eyes, milky and tired, revealed her undisguised knowledge and acceptance of knowing she would never see them again, not in her lifetime. She headed back inside her cabin leaving the night air no time to snatch away her breath the way it was taking away her boys. The row of cabins faced the edge of the woods and a river separated the two plantations. The woman's wooden door was swollen and warped, but her frail arms managed and lifted the ledge enough to drag it shut just as they disappeared into the night.

Sylvia looked away as young mothers comforted their crying babies and plugged their mouths shut with milk-filled breasts to fill their stomachs and quiet the noise. In the limited light of the moon, she felt her own breasts wasting away, useless and childless. Lu fell to her knees and wept. A monstrous emptiness seized her and she succumbed to the hopelessness of sorrow and sudden loneliness. Samson, a man with a lopsided limp, almost tripped over her in the darkness. Gathering himself, he stood listening on the opposite side of where Sylvia stooped rubbing Lu's back, because his short leg throbbed for relief from walking and because he understood loss and the grief it leaves to fill the space.

"She gon' be alright?"

"She gon' be fine. Just gon' take some time."

"Lost my boy a few years back. Got sold off one month to the day before 'mancipation came. Nearly cried myself to my death. Don't know where he end up. Dead o' alive. Think he far away from here, though. I know for sure soon as he learnt he was a free man, he would have come back here for us. 'Least to see 'bout his mama." Samson shook the thoughts out of his head and ran his hand over his tight-curled, almost beady hair.

Three women held hands as they passed, walking with heavy steps on the softened ground, sobbing. One stopped to touch Lu's arched and heaving back. "Bless your soul, Sister Lu. Bless your soul."

The innocent, sweet laughter of a child shot through the murmur of massive gloom. The gleeful sound quickened Sylvia and she thought to herself perchance the children knew best. She summed the adults focused on the remains, what was left behind—the empty bed, the extra cup, the over-filled kettle, the quiet floorboards and themselves, their worriment and their longing. How were they to cover their pain and ignore the empty space around them? How were they to find the good in it all when all the good they knew left them with scraps of themselves? All the years of wanting more, Sylvia thought, why were they not rejoicing? Them leaving was the good and the good of all the others who died without getting more.

Sylvia stood to her feet, stretching her back. She reached down for Lu's hand and pulled her up to stand. Samson sensed movement and strained his eyes to see in the dark night. "Lu, you just leave those tears right there." She could not see her hand in front her face but she found Lu's cheek and swiped away the tears. "Dry it up. No more crying."

"Sylvia, my boy is gone." Lu wept into her palms. "What am I gonna do?"

"Right now, you gon' stop that crying. Stop it!" She pulled at the locked fingers across her friend's face. "Now listen, just listen." Samson leaned in on the shorter of his two legs. "This night here, this is the night our people been waiting on. Dying and being killed for. You remember Arthur, from over on Butler?" Lu nodded but Sylvia could not see so she took the silence as a response. Lu wiped her eyes with the hem of her soaked apron. "You remember how he died?"

"Can't forget. Ground still holding his blood on some of the rocks."

"And you remember why he died?"

"Cause of those seeds. Gave 'em to Clary so she could plant her truck garden 'fore she died. White man say he stole 'em. I don't believe he did."

"The one thing his wife wanted to do. Plant something. Leave something behind before she left this world. She knew she probably wouldn't be here to look at it grow to harvest, sure enough. But planting 'em seeds was enough. Didn't live much too long after she put 'em in the ground to see the first sprout come up, but she planted it. And when it did, I went over there myself and sat with that curled up leaf. Tomato vine."

"That same vine over behind the...?"

"Same one." Sylvia reached for Lu's hand and took it in hers. "Everyone of us got a reason we here. And we ain't all here to see the flowers grow. Those that done planted every bit of hope and prayers and died for nights like this one we living in, to let you see your boy off into the free world, a free man, going somewhere he can have his own land and make a good life for him and his family. They done died for that, Lu." She squeezed her friend's hand in hers. "You think about all these tears you shedding for him to not go. If he don't go, he stay here. He gon' die here. And every bit of dream them children got that been planted in him by you, me, and everybody else that come 'fore us gone die right here with him."

"This here bigger than us." Samson said sucking in his bottom lip. "That's what you saying."

"That's what I'm saying. So Lu, you dry it up. Let God take care. He gon' watch over them and He gon' have mercy on them." She looked up at the sky dotted with starlight, Lu's hands still folded into hers. "He gon' have mercy on 'em."

There was a lamp in the distance moving through the darkness. They were not able to see who carried the light and knew for sure it was not one of them for they made certain to carry none. Just before sunrise, Lu had taken down the white sheet after hanging five days on the rope line. She hushed her crying and flung her head behind her as if she would be able to see her son and the others running farther and faster up the bank of the river and through the thick forest of trees before crossing the river at the border of the other plantation miles north of where they were. The uneven thumps of Samson's running feet sent an earnest plea to the others and they scurried. They knew their way through the darkness but the onset of sudden terror created chaos. They tugged each other, and those from the other plantation ran into whichever cabin was nearest to them. Sylvia and Lu stood motionless in spite of the excitement around them. They watched the light move across the field, glowing and beautiful, the way a star would on Earth. Then it disappeared as if swallowed up by the blackness. They stood there a while longer, still and at ease, until they heard the horses.

chapter 2

NELLA JO PRESSED HERSELF into the ivory porch column watching two townsmen on horseback ride up the path of the Butler Plantation. She was careful to hide the rise and fall of her small chest. White men can smell fear a mile away. The horses rode with vigor, their heads bobbed front and back in unison and purpose. Dirt lifted to a glorious, golden cloud as if something amazing was about to happen. But she knew better. Dealing with White folk was different from leading a land of Black folks who knew nothing more than themselves. Her feet mashed into the soles of the ankle boots Grayson had given her on returning from his last trip. With his arms around her waist, he had pulled her close, his thin lips pressed against her full, supple ones. She could have fallen from sheer satisfaction had he not been holding her. When he spun her around to see the shoes sitting on the chair, her heart could have jumped out of her chest. They were brand new. The shining silver fastener, she thought, would set her apart from the others and elevate her to be amongst the finer women of the town, the White ones. Gone for more than three months, she imagined his beard was grown into a puffy pillow, yellow and smooth. She could still feel the warmth of his face against her neck in the early hours of the morning and reassured herself he would return to her.

Nella Jo stood tall and stately on the porch as the round man walked over to where the square one stood, pulled a handkerchief from the pocket of his vest and wiped his glistening forehead.

"Step down here, gal," he said, folding his handkerchief. "Ain't proper for us to talk to you standing high up there. Your 'Mancipation Law be damned."

The other chuckled at the same time he pulled up the waist of his pants.

Her jaws clenched and her temples thumped. She maintained distance and remained near the base of the wide stairs.

"Your Master in town?" the square man spoke.

"Mr. Grayson Butler, sir," she said, "he's due back any day now."

"What day?"

"Can't say for certain."

It was not quite noon, yet the sun shut their eyes to slits.

"Well, what do you know about that Chewy's place back there in those cabins?" He pointed in the direction of the slave cabins.

The round man looked at Nella Jo from over the top of his specks. "She'd know nothing even if she knew something."

"Well, the only something I know, sir," she said, "is that Chewy's is a place for Blacks to get a meal and rest from a hard day's work." She tilted her head and held out her right hand, palm-up, as she'd seen Grayson do when making an obvious point. "A saloon, if you like, gentlemen."

"I wasn't talking to you, gal." Pellets of sweat rolled down his chubby cheeks onto the collar of his white shirt.

"Saloon, huh? New word you learned?" said the square man. "Why that Grayson Butler, with his uppity reading and writing slaves." He hacked tobacco spit at her ankle boots.

She did not look down but felt a sudden weight building on her foot.

Aiming for mischief he continued, "A rope and a tree wouldn't know the difference, though."

Nella Jo swallowed and shifted her eyes from the square man to the round one.

"When the last time you been back there?" asked the round man.

"About a week or so ago, sir." She folded her hands on her chest to make visible her clean nails, unstained by red clay and hoped the light breeze blew their way a whiff of the lilac oil she rubbed on her skin. "I'm not one to get back there much," she continued, "I have enough work to keep me busy right here."

The square man laughed. "Bed duty passing for work these days."

She saw his teeth and shivered in the sweltering sun.

"Listen here, gal," spat the round one, fed up, "You tell Butler we coming back here in a week's time." It took him two attempts to mount the gray mare, whose long, smoky tail slapped at flies. "And make sure to tell him that *saloon* you people running back there owes this town of Mercy taxes. You hear?"

"Yes, sir."

The horses trampled her words and she dropped her eyes on the spit, shiny and sprawled on her boot. She stomped her foot to fling the tobacco spit, the dishonor and humiliation. "You're mine and no one else's." Grayson told her when she was his slave. His washed out skin lying next to hers, he rubbed her all over for hours. "Never lower to shame." He told her. It made her shameful when he saw all of her, when he told her of her beauty, when his hand ran over the scar. It uneased her to hear him enjoy her, the disease turned to disbelief until, as time passed, she imagined herself not as he saw her but as she saw herself, like him. It was only then she opened her mind and took him in and forgot herself. With each stomp of her boot, she restored to herself airs and graces to erect her neck, straighten her back, enunciate her words and reenact the behavior she acquired through observation. Each illustrious, exaggerated and sometimes awkward refinement stocked her confidence and constructed salient features she was proud of.

"If only you'd arrived a moment sooner, I could have introduced you to the townsmen," she said to her daughter, Yuna, who approached from the side of the house.

"And why, Mother, would you do that?"

Nella Jo was standing tall and regal on the porch, looking as always in admiration of her daughter's golden complexion and the freckles on her fine nose. She thought her beauty would have eased the devilment in those men. Then she remembered the dark tunnel running through the square man's teeth.

"That was business I just handled. And, as the daughter of Grayson Butler, dear, you need to be groomed on how to handle such affairs." Nella Jo continued, even after Yuna had moved on to the back of the house. "I am not going to be here forever. You need to learn your father's business sooner than later!" When Yuna did not respond, she stepped down the porch steps after her. She knew the world would not of its own volition make way for Yuna to live in comfort in spite of her yellow skin and ability to read, write and add. "You need to take up the reigns, Yuna!" Nella Jo shouted. She looked around at the workers with the corners of her eyes, her chin high, her dress pulled up a slight degree and her back straight as a pole. "And you sure are as smart as any White woman when it comes to the books. Your daddy taught you hisself!" She wanted those around to hear and hoped they were reminded of their inferiority. "Listen to your mother!"

Yuna disappeared through the back door into the kitchen.

Why couldn't that girl be smarter with her choice of company? Nella Jo wondered while looking at the workers in the kitchen. In the sun, in her mind, her dress hoisted, a caul of dried spit on her boot, she thought there are people who lead and those who need to be led! Some are born to wash collards and to peel back the skin from immature potatoes. Others are born to carve away at fresh deer...

Nella Jo blinked at the deer eyes glaring at her from across the kitchen, at the thin red ropes of blood dripping from the wood table onto the floor.

"Absolute idiots!" she screamed, taking a step deeper inside the kitchen. "My floors are not for blood and gut stains—who's responsible? By God I will have her gutted, too."

Knives stopped. Everyone stopped what they were doing.

One young woman threw herself to the floor to scrub it with her own apron. Another grabbed a pile of cloth from beneath the kitchen's single window and rushed to help. The others raised their eyes just long enough to glance at the frenzy. A bowl of collards fell to the floor from the hands of an old woman.

"First Lady, please, forgib me? Please forgib me, First Lady? Forgib me, please First Lady?" The old lady begged. The soles of her shoes were worn and slanted.

"Shut up, you old fool and pick up that bowl!" Nella Jo snapped. "You're soon to be picked up by the Collector yourself, if I—"

"I'll get that," Yuna said to the old woman. Her voice sincere and urgent.

Nella Jo looked, terror on her face, as her daughter bent to pick up the bowl of collards and could not contain her restraint.

"Let the slave get it! Don't you get down there, Yuna! Get up!" She sped to the table.

Yuna stood, handed the bowl of collards to the old woman and made her way past her mother to the pile of potatoes being diced. The distraction allowed the workers enough time to lift the carcass off the table and carry it to the back door. Nella Jo watched them make certain a single drop of blood did not fall on her floor. One woman used her apron, another her dress, and another her own hand—a wide, aluminum basin in the other. The lash of her intimidation stirred frivolous delight and she broadened her mouth. When the door slammed behind them, she took one last glance at the remaining women, who kept their eyes fixed on their work.

"As you better," she said.

chapter 3

―――――

"Lord, don't let it be my boy."

"They had to cut the baby right out of her. Found the sac on the chicken coop fence. Still got blood in it."

"My Lord."

"Both of them? Both women?"

"Can't run long carrying somebody inside o' you. Sitting on top o' your bridge, ready to break you in half."

"Mavis say she dream last night 'bout her husband eyes. Say they sat there watching her. Didn't blink. Didn't do nothing. Just followed her everywhere she went doing her work."

"He should've never left her here."

"Said it was best he make way for them and he was gonna come back for her. We could just as well be going to this funeral for both they body parts if he'd plan it any other way."

"Well ain't no way my husband leaving this here place without me. We gone live together and die together. Where Mavis at anyhow? She gon' over already?"

"Sitting up in that cabin of hers, shaking and rocking. She ain't coming. Can't take knowing if any of them parts belong to him or not." The chatty woman shook her head. "I took her some pork soup and she made sure to tell me not to tell her a thing 'bout what I see over there tonight. Even if it is her husband. She just about begged me to keep my mouth shut."

"We all got to bear this one way or another. Ain't easy for none of us." A grunt hovered across a lazy wave riding alongside the raft. The aroma of hickory wood burning in the Butler smoke house sliced through the air. Sylvia admired a crow flying over. With jet black wings reaching for both ends of the sky, it floated carefree on air as they drifted across the water. She sat with Mistress' Bible entrusted to her laying across her lap. *"Take it! Can't be no right down there of blessing souls if there isn't a good book of God's word present. Take it, Silva." She whirled the mispronounced name from her throat within her appeal.* She sat thinking everyone and everything had their own way of getting to wherever they were headed. Some ways longer, required a little more strength, and some hard choices, but they went on in the way they knew how.

Lu was silent. Not a single tear filled her eyes as the rope slapped at the water and reeled the raft closer to the bank. Sylvia placed her own hand on her friend's. Lu flinched, declined the comfort and pulled hers away. Her dazed look told Sylvia she numbed herself and wanted to remain without feeling until she was sure who was who and what was what of the pieces of bodies found. With respect, Sylvia withdrew her hand and prayed inside herself for everyone, whole and those torn to pieces.

Three nights came and left since the first of the body parts began appearing. The scream traveled through walls, doors and windows and woke up all of Mercy the morning Holly Mae walked outside her cabin door and stepped on a foot with no body. It had been half wrapped in the cloth of a shirt she had made with her own hands for her uncle a week before he'd left for Hartha Gables. It sat severed in front of her until her husband ran all the way from the cane fields to his wife. She knew her own stitching. Her sobs filled the quarters as older women and children rushed out to see what happened. Those closest to Holly Mae's cabin rushed the children back inside when they caught sight of the amputated foot laying out in the open for all to see. Once her husband moved her back inside, he went back out for the foot and picked it up with his bare hands for it was his family. He rewrapped the foot and carried it to the elder's cabin, where the transition from Earth life to the next life would be completed.

Not long after, Sylvia watched a man lift the fainted body of a girl sent to fetch water from the well who pulled up two fingers, a forearm, and a thick column of flesh resembling a neck in her pail. Pieces and parts of friends and family members headed for Hartha Gables were strewn from Purvis to Butler and placed where they were sure to be found by those who loved them most.

And then there were the pieces of people no one knew or could identify. Whose child had the pointed nose with light freckles found in the chicken coop?

"My God, even the ones with White in 'em?"

"They go through whatever to kill the Black part!"

"But couldn't they see the child had White inside?"

"Inside the same ain't it?"

To whom did the half scraped bone, maybe a knee or an elbow, once belong to? And the tongue? And the single leg with the penis still in place, sole of the feet thick as a potato?

Sylvia was the last of the women to be helped from the raft tied to two large stacks hammered deep into the soggy ground. "Go on," she shooed Lu ahead of her onto the Butler Plantation. It was a steep climb to the slave cemetery and with the help of sheer will and stable rocks she and the others made it to the top.

There were all the remains on a large piece of muslin. On it, laid all the answers to the questions they hauled since the chilly night in which they sprang up lying flat on floor boards, pulled from behind cabins and trees screaming and falling all over each other in the dark while chasing the horses as they trampled the lush, damp grass racing for the river in search of their people on the run. An ear still pierced with the most beautiful wooden hoop earring Sylvia had ever seen. Every woman on Purvis had admired it and dreamed of a pair being slipped around their own bare lobes. None had a husband as skilled with smoothing away the slightest bump in any stalk of wood to create the most perfect adornment. The woman who lost her ear, Glory, had been beautiful, some would say the most beautiful black woman on all of Purvis and Butler plantations. The night she and her husband left for Hartha Gables, wives were exuberant in secret for the temptation she presented to their own husbands was leaving. Now, there she was at their feet, a piece of herself, still beautiful, and they felt their insides sink due to their selfishness and wished they would have prayed for her harder.

"Let us therefore draw near with confidence to the throne of grace..."

She clutched the Bible to her bosom, chin digging into chest. She thought of Mistress. It was because of her Sylvia had become a believer. Those mysterious words in the Hebrew chapter became her daily prayer, even before she fully understood the meaning of them.

She did not consider herself a Christian, but trusted the writings of the sacred book. *"I'm black and I'm a woman. That there is enough for me to handle, Mistress. Your religion got too many rules and things to remember to do and say and this and that. All the energy and life I got left in me going I'm saving up for just keeping myself alive. If I be a good person, that'a take care of all that other stuff."* She wanted to feel the bend of dough against her palms and the dusty leaves of a pocket full of herbs in her apron from her morning picking. Those were her wants. Sylvia prayed to wake up to a body still in one piece and half way working each time Julius beat her into the floor...and if she did not wake, she prayed to go to a Heaven where she could one day be reunited with her boys. Those things were enough.

Someone shushed the whispers hovering between the live oak trees as the burial went on into the late evening. Another grunted and sucked their teeth. The elder continued praying in the old language under the start of the waning moon. Sylvia looked down at her feet, still attached to her own body. Worn as they were, her feet had life running through them. She did not understand what the sounds meant coming from the prayer in the old language. What she did know for sure was God did not play around with who he called to Heaven, when He called them, and in how many pieces. For His reason, it was their time. With the others, she kept a bowed head.

"...that we may receive mercy and may find grace to help in time of need."

One hole, the size Sylvia dug many times for making outside cooking fires, sunk into the earth. The elder and younger man wearing her same sunken eyes and wide nose, helped lower her to her knees as she folded the muslin over the parts. She was old and unstable and a severed finger fell from the muslin and hit the earth. It was then a frantic scream shattered the quiet.

Mavis had come.

Like everyone else, she could no longer stand not knowing. She needed to know just as bad as she wanted to remain blind. It was her husband's finger. By the knot she had rubbed to sooth many nights, she identified her husband. A displaced joint twisting the finger in a peculiar, distinguished way, summoned Mavis. She pushed past others to drop to her knees at the finger in the earth where grass neglected. With a raise of the elder woman's frail hand to the young man, he and all of them left Mavis to weep. It was only right to allow her this moment. If not, all the sorrow would grow inside of her and be blamed the reason for her own too soon death. Mavis' tears filled her palms cupped over her face and passed through her fingers. The dear elder woman rubbed at her back for as long as the tears came and the cries made melody into the evening. When there was silence, aside from Mavis, the elder woman continued to fold the muslin cloth, slow and particular. She did not reach for the finger in front of Mavis. She tied the bundle of the remains with a hay cord. She laid it in the deepest part of the grave, said a final prayer and turned to reach for the hand of her boy to climb again to her feet.

It was over. Two men began shoveling the dirt into the hole, singing as they worked. The crowd went in their own directions humming the same hymn. There was nothing more to be sought. Nothing more to dream. For many, no one would return for them not even themselves. It was back to work with the same heavy satchel in their hearts, only heavier.

When the final shovel of dirt was patted into place, of the few remaining, Sylvia and Lu embraced, thankful no parts of Lu's family had been buried. Lu headed back to the raft and left Sylvia to her thoughts and prayers. When Sylvia had seen her friend off, she placed a hand on the shoulder of Mavis and a few others who had planted themselves on the ground to mourn. She took her time heading back to the raft and what awaited on Purvis. Sylvia was also thankful for a little time off she'd gotten to go across the river for the burial. Mistress had been in strange sorts all day—by late morning, Sylvia could already feel the choke of air between Mistress and Master Purvis. Nothing new. Sylvia'd rather have had a different reason for the time off, but was grateful just the same to be away from the fight brewing between those two hate birds.

Passing the main house, Sylvia heard glass crashing and hurried like a jack rabbit past the open dining-room window, already knowing the mess spilling on the other side of those walls. They may have been the biggest walls on any house she had ever seen, but they did not hold in all the fussing Mistress and Master Purvis tried to hide when they stepped out the front door. Sylvia had cleaned just as much sadness in her own two-room, clapboard cabin as she had in the Purvis' oversized dining room, two parlors, and all six bedrooms upstairs. A heart's broken pieces did not need so many empty bedrooms to lay across. Grief piled up like dust waiting for Sylvia to do something about it. And what was that something? Mistress insisted Sylvia change the unused bedding and place fresh flowers in each room every week. "Clean bedding and fresh life," Mistress would say. "It keeps the rooms feeling loved." Of course. Sylvia could not recall a time Master Purvis had ever given Mistress a single flower.

After a while, the silence that rode the air between the main house and the cookhouse gripped Sylvia by the throat. She tugged at the double-knot of her apron at the back of her neck, then leaned against the old kitchen door for air to stare out into another night. At times like these, the cookhouse suffocated what was left of her life, calling up heat and sweat.

The dough began to rise from the wooden board, stretching its skin, growing into itself. The air thickened at the same time Mistress let out a scream, causing Sylvia to knock the rolling pin from the table, sending flour everywhere. She crouched to the floor to clean up the mess. It was only a matter of time before she would be in the main house, in the same position, scrubbing away Master Early Purvis' anger from the floors and walls.

Sylvia shooed a gnat away from her nose. The bread was ready, brown top arched and split open.

chapter 4

———⸙———

LONELINESS MAKES ONE MISERABLE and misery, a silent maladjustment of the mind, takes over in small movements until it devours even the eyes. Nella Jo sat at the window of her bedroom gazing out at the live oak tree hanging low to the ground. She watched the bushy-tailed squirrels chasing each other when they played. It made her think there was not a single person with whom she had shared such moments of glee and carefree living. As a child she had one brother and he was determined to leave, not her, but the confinements of slavery. So, as often as he could, he tried to escape even without shoes on his feet. Each time he tried, the two of them grew farther apart for when he returned, he was busy plotting and growing angry. It was during these times, she was busy hardening her heart to him until she grew to dislike him.

In a handheld mirror, she gazed into her own sunken eyes surrounded by short, thin lashes. She smiled at her reflection. Her bold, red painted lips disguised the smallness of her and fooled many slaves into believing, as she did, her life was near perfection. She was despised and envied by many, and the curiosity all over their faces pleased her. Their attention fed and propelled her, yet she was still unsatisfied. She had embraced her place, well aware of the advantages. Still days like the one she begrudged the squirrels reminded her of what she does not have and had given up without enough attention to the loss. Young and innocent, she began ruling the slaves with force and distaste forgetting she was one herself. Neglecting all others, she was content with Grayson. He was all she desired, needed and wanted.

She pulled the sheer curtains together and huffed. Flopped on the side of the bed in the small room behind the kitchen, she was her own company in the space big enough to hold the many nights she shared with her dear Grayson. In there, she was allowed to simply be, although in being, she was just as alone as she was on the other side of the heavy door with the pewter latch. No friends, scraps of a family, and a lover of the man she loved except beyond the plantation – and except in the presence of guests.

She kept a distance between herself and the others. She was their master and they her slaves. It was within the same distance her daughter grew to dislike her and her ways. Once a little, golden girl with spiral locs of hair hugging her oval face, she was no longer a baby, or even a child. She had her own mind, her own desires, her own opinions, the exact things keeping the distance between the two of them. Yuna found pleasure in service in spite of her father and mother's efforts to deter her from it. The thought alone turned Nella Jo's stomach beneath the bodice as she headed for the kitchen. As soon as she opened the door, two women, one appearing the same age as her own nineteen year old Yuna, ceased their laughter and lowered their eyes stepping aside in the dim hallway. Nothing in Nella Jo expected them to strike up a conversation and tell her about the mundane details of their day, yet the freeze of their steps stuck at her the way icicles jabbed into the ground when they fall from the tree outside her window. She taught herself long ago to disallow such things from shattering her to pieces, but a part of her, the part which did not forget the first time her brother, whom she loved, ran away was well aware of the pain.

Yuna sat at the kitchen table working.

"Good afternoon." Nella Jo's smile, the real one, not the one from the mirror, covered her face. It was a rare smile she seldom used and kept to moments with her daughter and her dear Grayson. He had been the first and only one to ever tell her her smile warmed winters for him. Yuna glanced at her mother who stood in perfect poise in the center of an empty kitchen in the middle of the day. "And how are we?"

"I'm fine, Mother."

Nella Jo hoped for more words to trail behind the stale ones even though she did not know what they should be. The silence between them was frigid and sturdy, and growing. Taking a cup from the collection, she poured water from the kettle. She strained the tea leaves and sat across from Yuna at the table stirring sugar into the steaming liquid. Not a single word crossed the table until Nella Jo could no longer take the awkward silence and forced the conversation to begin.

"So Yuna, how are things with your Aunt Sylvia?

Yuna did not care to discuss anything with her mother.

"Has there been any word from my father?"

The change of topic took Nella Jo by surprise as she turned the hot liquid to her face, steam rushing from the cup.

"Not a word."

"Please let me know when you receive word from him." Yuna stood to leave the table, drying her hands on the apron made of a material of a lower quality than Nella Jo's grandeur dress. As she turned to walk out the back door, in a last call, Nella Jo raised her hand. "Yuna. How...how is your grandmother?"

"Mother, she lives in the same cabin you stuffed her in years ago. You know the way." She left the kitchen and walked outside.

———◦◦◦———

Nella Jo knew guns with the same familiarity she knew money and comfort. Master Butler taught her to shoot a target, still or moving, right around the same time he had hired a tutor from another town to teach Yuna to read and write. It was his dream to one day send his child off to school to learn all there was to learn out in the world, free of boundaries which plague an ignorant mind. What he also desired was a woman able to handle herself, protect his only child and his plantation while he was away if things ever got out of hand.

She stared down the small hole of the rear sight, waiting for it to disappear and the front sight to take over her vision. Her breath was relaxed as though washing her hands or having a tea biscuit in the afternoon. Without a thought, she exhaled, and pulled the front trigger, ignoring the second, that was Grayson's. The baby chick's body splattered to pieces across the coop and wired fence.

"Dammit." She said the words under her breath, pointing the butt to the ground. She pulled out the metal tipped ramrod and used it to load her next bullet. Satisfied she lifted the gun and positioned it again on her shoulder. With one eye shut, Nella Jo held the gun steady and aimed at another chick pecking away at what remained of the last target. "Here chicky, chicky." She amused herself. It was the way she had heard her daughter call out to the helpless and useless birds many mornings, tossing feed around. It was only the ones able lay eggs she valued, and there were enough of them. The babies served no purpose to her either, they took up space and took food away from the hens. "Here chicky, chick…"

"Ah, 'scuse me ma'am."

She swung her entire self around, eye still to the barrel and finger on the trigger. It was Chewy. She continued her aim at him.

With his hands to the sky, he jumped, "Wo, wo. Its just me. I don't mean no harm."

She lowered the gun to the ground and chuckled. "Sure you don't."

Chewy lowered his hands and reached slowly in his pocket. He pulled out the dollar bills and fanned them towards her. "See. See here. Just came to bring you what I owe ya. That's all." He poked the top portion of his body out towards her with his hand. The rest of him stayed planted firm. "No harm."

"You couldn't bring me harm even if you wanted to." She rubbed at a smudge on the side of the barrel. "How much money you have there?"

"What you asked for and a lil bit more for your troubles, for waitin' an' all."

She was annoyed he seemed pleased with himself as if he had done her a grand favor. He owed her ever bill of the money and more. And she had had to wait, and waiting for her money had not been a part of their agreement when he asked her a few months ago if he could turn the old sew house into a drink place. The sew house had not been used in years and was serving no use other than collecting pine straw and rats. Nella Jo thought the same of his proposal as Chewy had of the sew house—there was money to be made off of it. Easy money, requiring nothing of her. She told him how much of his profit she expected for herself. He had reached his hand to shake on the deal the way he had seen White folk do in business. She looked at his hand as the filthy extension of the big, sweaty man he was and walked back into the Butler house.

So now there he was, days late on their agreement expecting her to do a jig because he threw in a little bit extra. "Let me see that." She snatched the bills from his hand and counted them. "This is what 'usual business' money looks like, huh?"

"More or less."

"Um huh." She'd finished counting the money and stuffed the folded bills into her dress pocket. Placing the barrel back up to her shoulder, she eyed the target again. This chick, a bit bigger than the first, waddled. Nella Jo steadied her aim, locking her lower body into a stance. "There's trouble coming your way."

"What's that you say, ma'am?"

"You heard me." She kept her eye beaming down the shaft. "It might do you some good to keep up that 'usual' business you've got going on over there to be able to take care of things."

"I don't quite get what you saying."

Nella Jo put the gun down, nettled, pointing the barrel back to the ground. Chewy pulled out his cloth from his overall pocket and wiped away the terror the gun being upright was sending through him. "Listen here. White folk aren't taking well to the idea of you running that place down there and not giving them their cut of what you're making."

"But its outright my money. My place, my money." he declared. "'sides, I been paying you. You give me Master Butler word I can open my place and not be messed with."

"All money is White money. Soon enough, these few dollars you're giving me won't be enough to keep much of anybody happy, especially the white men in town. They want their share, too."

"I'm barely covering your share."

"Not my problem. I'm just telling you what I know."

Chewy dug his big hands down into his pockets, a grown man's pout. She thought he looked helpless with too much hair on his head and face. Yellow eyes like two gold coins sitting in his head. "What you reckon I do?"

He was a fool trying to run a business, she thought. She was sure it was his wife who told him when to fall asleep and when to breathe. "Master Butler will be back soon. Those townsmen will tell him about your place and how they want their share for taxes and whatever else they can come up with. You're on Butler property, and you're making money. Of course Master Butler will come looking for you to pay them. You need to figure out your plan between now and then. White men want their share of your money, not your talk."

"Well like I said, I'm barely making enough to pay you."

"And like I said, that problem belongs to you. Not me." She put the butt of the gun back on her shoulder without another word. Chewy stood there watching as she took her aim, finished with the heavy news she had just shot his way.

"Guess I'll be goin'," he said, both relieved and anxious to get away from her warnings and her gun.

Nella Jo kept her aim. "Mind what I tell you. And there's no harm in showing your thankfulness for me giving you a jumpstart on what's brewing." He knew what she meant. Chewy dug deep into his pocket again and laid another dollar bill on the stoop next to where she stood. Before long, he realized she had no more words for him. She was satisfied with what he gave her and gave him her silence to lead him back down the hill to the cabins where he belonged.

She continued on with her afternoon entertainment, a combination of releasing her frustrations towards Yuna and the rest of the world, and simply being bored in her aloneness.

"I see you little chic-chic. I see you."

"Mother!"

Nella Jo nearly dropped the gun at the sound of Yuna's horrified shout.

"What are you doing?" Yuna looked over at the six balls of blood stains strewn across the chicken pen. The few chicks remaining huddled in a corner by a hen. "Have you lost every bit of your mind!?"

Nella Jo questioned her tone. She was the mother and despite her age and their poor excuse for a relationship, Yuna was still the daughter. Yuna rushed to the wire fence and undid the latch. She laid her palms against the sides of her face in dismay. Nella Jo watched her daughter's dramatic performance wondering why it was so necessary. There would be more chicks. Probably by tomorrow. That was why eggs were laid. "Stupid girl! Too much emotion will be the death of her one day. Too much heart," Nella Jo mumbled to herself, un-cocking the rifle.

"They're chicks." Nella Jo called out to her distraught daughter.

"They're dead! You killed them!" Yuna sat on the bare ground amidst the crimson spots already baking into the ground. A tiny beak in her hand, tears welled in her eyes.

Nella Jo walked over. "I can't believe you're actually crying. Get up from there, Yuna." She leaned into the fence. "You're making a spectacle of yourself. Get up right now!"

"Go away!"

"I will not." Nella Jo raised her chin high, the firm way women did when they were standing their ground. "You get up from there this instance!"

"Oh die, Mother!"

"Yuna! I'll have you not speak to me like some ill-mannered child! Straighten yourself up!"

"Mother." Yuna stared through narrowed eyes at her mother. "I am not a baby nor am I a child. These...," she opened her palm and shoved the bloodied beak in Nella Jo's face. "These were babies! These were babies that you killed! And why?"

"You'll watch your tone and get that filth away from me." She took a step back.

"These were innocent lives. Have mercy on your horrible, horrible soul!" Yuna pushed past Nella Jo and stormed off to the back of the kitchen house, tossing the beak at her mother's foot. "You will pay for this, Mother! One way or another, God will not forget what you've done!"

For a moment, the words stung more than the sun rays beaming on her. When she looked behind her, she saw the living chicks, still pecking in a corner. At her feet the eyes bulged from the head of a dismantled baby bird staring up at her empty and alone self.

chapter 5

THE COOKHOUSE WAS FILLED with the aroma of salt-pork and sour dough, all wrapped in the earthy fragrance of lemon, thyme, and fresh garlic. Mistress had announced the coming of her mother-in-law through bloody and swollen lips followed by tears days earlier.

"You're going to need to get in there and clean up that awful mess Vivian's made in the dining room." The order fell from the slit in a melon face with bulging eyes behind a pair of twisted, round glasses.

"Will do, Master Purvis." Sylvia eased through the small space between him and the entryway.

He straightened his glasses with one hand, then was gone, stepping wide towards the stables.

The dining room looked worse than last time. The painting of Master and Mistress was knocked off balance. An entire row of the crystal figurines Mistress collected since she was a young girl was shattered. Every little angel rested with either a broken wing or a missing head.

It took a while for Sylvia to reach Mistress' room—because of all the items tossed about the stairs and floor—but when she did, she saw Mistress had not bothered to clean herself. There she was, on the floor, back propped against the bed. Blush-faced, she stared at Sylvia's feet. Dried blood streaked the side of her face. Her lip had grown inside out, kneaded and baked by Master's hand. Sylvia dabbed a cloth with water from the pitcher on the nightstand and knelt beside the shattered woman to blot the gash near her eye. Mistress winced, sucked in her swollen lip, and refused to look at her devout maidservant, her dear friend.

"No. Don't do that," Sylvia said applying tender touches, then folded the damp cloth over and dabbed again. She looked up at Sylvia, an internal struggle apparent in her eyes, trying to remember how to continue living in her own body. Sylvia understood all too well the absence of words between them and remembered the many times she would also leave herself, whether under the hand of her own husband or Master Purvis himself. She and Mistress may not run off to the same quarters in their minds, but they both ran just the same.

"Silva," Mistress said lacking strength, "have you noticed how the tulips are coming in this year? Do you think they're supposed to be as pale as they are?" Glossed-over eyes stared back at the door. "I expected them to be more lively and more full. Didn't you?"

"Yes ma'am. I sure did."

There was no more for either of them to say about the flowers below the open bedroom window where their scent, alive and sweet, begged to differ. Neither of them cared about tulips or bread or white shirts in this moment. It was a way in and out of the reality of the night for Mistress to enter and exit without notice. Sylvia always noticed.

Finally, Mistress looked Sylvia in the eye. "I can't believe you still have that limp. Hasn't it been over a month now? One day, Silva, we're both going to be able to walk straight and upright and look at ourselves in a mirror without shedding tears."

"Maybe. Don't think it's gonna be on this side of Heaven, though."

"Oh, but it will be!" No sooner had the words slipped from Mistress' swollen lip did she sink back into her sadness. *"It's just going to take a little time."*

After a heavy breath, Mistress picked up the pages of a letter without really looking at them. *"Silva, we're going to need extra butter for Sunday,"* she said as if business could heal her wounds. *"You know how Early's mother loves your sweet-cream butter."*

In the twenty years Mistress had been married to Master Purvis, his mother had visited only a few times—but there was always hell to be paid the minute Mrs. Purvis stepped foot on the plantation. At the thought of her waving her fancy, laced hand fan, making sweet-cream butter was the least of Sylvia's concerns.

"Just how much butter are we gonna need?" she asked, her chest already tightening.

Mistress looked at her with red-rimmed eyes, ready to leap. Shaking the letter, she yelled, *"A whole week's worth! She's even going to be here for the party."* Then she sobbed and flung the pages to the floor.

Bitter and sour as Mrs. Purvis was, she loved her bread sweet and her meat spicy. If she tasted and felt the food to be bland, she would demand it be prepared to her liking. "Oh, no, I need to see the herbs!" She would say. Sylvia and the kitchen staff would hurry to remake whatever she requested. Although bread cannot be rushed, dough always sat ready and extra meat laid in wait already pounded until the fibers loosened to pull in seasonings.

Mistress stood at the doorway, amused with Sylvia imparting her skills to the new squinting and giggling girl she acquired a year ago.

There were many times Mistress marveled at the joyous friendship Negro women shared. They were easy in their way with each other without the need for pretense the way it was at parties and meetings with other society wives.

"Be careful you don't get none of this in your eye the way I did once." Red juice ran down the side of Sylvia's hands and arms. "Now cover the meat with the chili paste like this, and it's ready to go on the fire."

Mistress was not sure she liked Dollet's playful ways and she hoped Silva and Nan, the cookhouses' main cook, would have her contain it in the kitchen. When Mistress caught a glimpse of the glint in her young eyes and bright teeth she lost all warmth about their camaraderie. Every new girl could be a rose to a master and a thorn in the side of his wife. She married her husband when she was eighteen years old with porcelain skin and a shiny head of hair. A blossoming woman, ripe and beautiful, and even then his eyes wandered, and rested on pretty young slaves. She grew up without wealth but with money and was taught to not look down on any human being in spite of their meager stock. Therefore, she was trained to see a person as a person, a man a man and woman a woman. She grew knowing everything she had as a woman every other woman had, every bit the same. And so, a slave was a slave but a woman first – a beauty first, soft skin first, a tender lover first. Intimidation was not the prick, possibility was.

Before Mistress made her presence known in the cookhouse, she heard the girl say something about chili and a new husband's privates, and then laughed to tears along with Nan. Mistress almost laughed, too, until she saw how the woven horsehair necklace the girl said the new husband had given her trembled on her young breasts.

Just then, the women looked up and noticed Mistress standing there, looking somewhere between mirthful and angry. Sylvia cleared her throat and said, too loudly, "In all my years of working in the cookhouse, I never made the mistake of gettin' any kinda pepper in my eye."

The girl winked as if Mistress were one of them. "Don't you worry 'bout me and that chili, Ms Sylvia, I'm learnin'."

Sylvia slid past the girl she adored and placed under her wing, and approached Mistress. "Mistress, I done taught Dollet here how to make you and Master's supper, even a whole feast for Mrs. Purvis."

"You just be careful with that knife," said Mistress, seriously, sending all four women into a round of giggles.

"I'm getting used to it, ma'am," the girl said to Mistress. "Them yams last night just about broke my wrist. Doing these greens is nothing."

"Going 'round back to wash up, Mistress. Then it'll be 'bout time for me to show my face inside. Mrs. Purvis gon' have all kind of trash-talkin' for you if she want for anything more than a few minutes."

Nan looked at the stream of dried chili juice on Sylvia's arms. "You better go and get that off you before it turn you inside out. Them peppers ain't nothin' to play with."

<hr>

At the annual Purvis party, Sylvia stood patiently beside the overdone table filled with drinks and hors d'oeuvres. The pungent smell of Whiskey floated out of the mouths of Mercy's wealthiest men and filled every corner of the parlor. The stench overpowered the evening fragrance of lavender outside the open window. Judging from the numerous times Mistress dabbed the handkerchief over her forehead, Sylvia figured the scent of cigar sickened her along with the painted smile she forced herself to wear all night. From the corner where Sylvia stirred a crystal punch bowl of Savannah Tea, she could hear Master Purvis' whisper into his wife's ear.

"Do not start that tonight, Vivian."

Sylvia saw his grip on her arm and guessed he was making poor Mistress sicker by his position in her face, the odor flowing out of his mouth and into her. He downed the last of his drink with a tilt of his head, and before the last drop slid from the glass or Sylvia could rush to replenish it, he gestured for Dollet to bring over a refill. Sylvia lost count of how many glasses he had, but knew he was long past too many. She had also lost track of all the wives' idle chitchat with Mistress about cloth patterns and the already blazing heat of spring while their husbands discussed the latest plantation robberies, the ever-rising price of tea, and what needed to be done about Chewy's, the moonshine place over on the Butler Plantation.

"Who knows what kind of money they have running through there. We're letting them get an upper hand on running a business, and it's a downright crime, if I do say so myself."

"Well, the taxes should be taken out of that Grayson Butler. It's his land, his Negros!"

"If you can ever catch him in town. He leaves that plantation at the hand of his nigger wench. A disgrace."

"I hear she's got a firm hand on those Negros, though, I tell you. She keeps her own palms greased."

"With money that should damn well be ours!"

"Calm down! Calm down!"

"Calm down? How can I calm down when these Negros are sucking us dry? We 'freed' them. And now we're going to let them live on our land and make our money. It's a crime!"

"It is not a crime. It's just not right—but it sure isn't a legitimate crime by anybody's law."

"Well, crime or no crime, they're getting out of control."

"Sure enough. Cut them at the knees. And the wrists."

"I want my share of it! I kept my slaves well and fed. They owe me what's mine! Hell, they owe every goddamn Master that's been good to them in the whole damn town of Mercy!

When Dollet took Master Purvis another half full glass into the circle of angry men, an awkward silence shot into her as she walked away with the tray of empty glasses. The circle parted as if someone had called them back to their posts, and Master Purvis took Mistess' arm, again, under his own in what Sylvia knew was a false display. She continued to stir the punch, stealing frequent looks at the couple. Her quick heartbeat was mirrored in Mistress' unsteady eyes and the nod she gave to the mayor's wife walking pass.

"This don't look like its gone be a good night for Mistress, Ms. Sylvia," Dollet whispered, easing to the other side of the table to fill more glasses.

Sylvia frowned. "You go on up and get her bed ready. Nan and I can handle things down here for a little while."

"Yes ma'am."

Just as Sylvia turned back, Master Purvis was making his way over to a group of men standing near the door to the serving room. Her eyes searched for Mistress and found her leaning behind a high-backed chair near the window. A late breeze moved the new curtain around her. She managed to make her way across the parlor without calling attention to herself and her speed, but Mrs. Purvis had already reached Mistress. The two, a pair to watch interact with each other, had been civil to each other all evening. Mrs. Purvis had arrived in a chatty mood and Mistress had obliged her in conversation and tea on the front porch while the house staff prepared the house for the party. The interaction was abnormal and Sylvia knew it was only a matter of time before it would come to an end, she only hoped it wasn't tonight. Mrs. Purvis swayed her way across the parlor reaching Mistress seconds before Sylvia could rescue her.

"Quite the party. Don't you think?" Mrs. Purvis pushed away the heat of the night waving her small hand fan around her. Sylvia took care to stop in her tracks, careful not to interrupt. "Vivian, dear? Vivian?"

Mistress held on to the curtain, which Sylvia hoped would stay as she caught Nan's eye, who stood near the table with her hands folded in wait for guest requests. Following Sylvia's gaze, Nan saw Mistress' hand fan sitting on the other side of the room and, like a true heroine, headed for it. By the time Nan reached Sylvia, Mistress had slid down into the seat.

"Vivian?" Mrs. Purvis hissed. "What is the matter with you? Are you plum drunk? This chair is designated for the men!"

"Let's get you upstairs, Mistress," Sylvia said. With Nan's help, she tried to stand the woman up.

"Vivian!" Mrs. Purvis hissed again. "This does not look good. You cannot just leave a party you are hosting with my son!" Her handfan flicked back and forth as if trying to fan away the embarrassment.

Mistress' face was the color of chili as she stood lacking stability.

"Vivian Purvis! These are the most important people in Mercy! Do hold yourself together for the sake of the Purvis name." Mrs. Purvis looked from Sylvia to Nan as though they were a part of a scheme to ruin the party.

"Gal." Master Purvis held his empty glass up above the crowded room and yelled clear across the parlor as Dollet returned from upstairs. "Why don't you trot yourself on over here and bring me another one."

"Oh dear God! Have both of you lost all sense of decency?" Mrs. Purvis stormed off in the direction of her drunken son.

Sylvia and Nan were glad for the opportunity to escort Mistress to the parlor door, almost clear of anyone's attention—until Master Purvis crossed right in front of them, wobbling. They quickly let go of Mistress' hands, and like her husband, she teetered. Master Purvis' bulging eyes narrowed from the round rim of his spectacles.

"What'd I tell you, Vivian?" He slurred. "You'll not embarrass me tonight. So, you pull yourself together this instant for the mayor and his wife..."

He grabbed an equally unsteady Mistress by the arm. It seemed to Sylvia his reach was more for steadying his own balance. She saw the mayor's wife a few feet away, already complimenting Mistress about the party, and before either Sylvia or Nan could stall the approaching couple, Mistress slid from her husband's grasp to the floor.

After the gasps and concerns faded to whispers and contemptuous looks, the party guests requested their coats and called for their wagons. Mrs. Purvis stepped over Mistress' body still sprawled out on the parlor floor.

"Early Purvis, have you no etiquette left in you? It would be you I'd expect to uphold some dignity at this party since clearly this, this…ill excuse of a wife of yours has made a fine rug of herself in the middle of the floor." She glanced down at her daughter-in-law, then at Sylvia and Dollet, both kneeling at Mistress' side, fanning and dabbing her face.

He turned the glass up to his head and emptied it. "What is the trouble now, Mother? Am I not standing here next to my wife as you ordered only an hour ago."

"Your guests!" Mrs. Purvis spoke through clinched teeth and stretched her eyes to a bulge at her son. It was the first time Sylvia had ever witnessed the woman saying anything in a way that did not beg for attention. "Your guests are leaving. Goodbyes and pardons are in order, don't you think?"

Master Purvis nudged the empty glass down at Dollet's shoulder for her to take it. Sylvia took the damp towel from her and continued wiping Mistress' forehead.

From the front door, Sylvia could hear his voice carrying all the way to the parlor. "Yes, she'll be fine. It must be something she ate. Thank you for your concern. See you at the next party." Finally, the door slammed shut. Master Purvis' heavy feet stomped into the stairs, heading to bed.

"Early Purvis!" Mrs. Purvis screeched again.

"Yes Mother. What is it now?" His stomping stopped halfway to the top.

"Aren't you forgetting something?"

With a slight chuckle, he returned, "Oh yes. Where is my head? How could I have forgotten. Goodnight, dear Mother. Oh, and I love you." He continued up the stairs, closing his bedroom door behind him, leaving his unconscious wife on the floor.

Sylvia looked at Nan, who was looking at Dollet, who stared at Mrs. Purvis with such intensity she missed the hand motion Sylvia made trying to distract her from such an inappropriate gaze. Mrs. Purvis headed towards the stairs. "Sylvia, be a dear and get her up from there before morning. It would indeed ruin another day to have to see her lying there that way without truly being as dead as she looks."

Dollet carried Mistress' legs while Nan locked her hands under Mistress' arms. "Be careful."

"We being careful. You just get the door open so we can put her right in the bed." Nan huffed.

"She can't go to bed in her party clothes, Nan." Sylvia came back. "We have to get her out of this dress at least."

"Look here. I'm getting her up these stairs and into that bed. Then I'm going back down these same stairs to get to work on all the cleaning gotta get done tonight 'fore I can go home and go to sleep. Now what you do with her once I put her in this bed is up to you. But I don't plan to stay here 'til morning. So what she wear to bed ain't the least bit of my concern."

Dollet snickered at Nan and the expression her words left on Sylvia's face. Both women shot a chastising glance at the girl and her laughter ceased. "Hush the noise out there, for God sake!" Master Purvis yelled from his room. The women got Mistress in the room and before Sylvia could get the covers settled just right, Nan was heading back out the door pulling Dollet with her by the wrist.

Sylvia removed the hair pin from Mistress' sleeping head to give her comfort. The last time she had had one of her spells, not nearly as bad as this one, she woke up with an awful headache, nausea and with awful fever lasting two days. It was already made up in her mind she could not leave Mistress alone in this condition. What if this time she awoke in worse shape than before? Already, she'd been out longer than any other time she had fainted. And her head, Mistress took a pretty rough bang against the hard wood floor. Sylvia thought again of all the restricting clothes and jewelry the sleeping woman was still wearing and how they would not make for easy resting. Pulling back the covers, she started with the fastener on the ankle boots, silver and shiny.

Night was turning to day when Sylvia saw Mistress open her eyes somewhere in the dim candlelight. The nickel-sized bump on Mistress' head was fresh, but it matched the old one beneath Sylvia's headscarf. Mistress blinked her way back to consciousness several times while Sylvia opened the curtains wider, allowing dawn's air to stir into the top level of the house. She was back at Mistress' bedside, wringing a cloth and placing it across her head for the umpteenth time.

Mistress tried to sit up. "My Lord, what hour is it? You should be home by now, Silva."

"And leave you here for dead? No, ma'am." Sylvia eased Mistress back onto the pillow. "I'm right where I'm supposed to be. Besides, nothing waiting for me at home that can't keep on waiting."

"Julius?" Mistress said behind closed lids.

"Drunk. Probably fast asleep." Sylvia sighed. "If anything, you and your spell save me from a new limp. Besides, I'd rather be here."

"You're too kind to me." She patted Sylvia's lap. "I just don't want any extra trouble for you. Especially on my account."

Sylvia gave a sigh and shook her head.

A while later, when morning was complete, Sylvia sat in the chair across from Mistress' bed, dozing. The slam of the door downstairs jerked her awake. She knew Master Purvis was off to town to handle affairs. Sylvia rose from the chair to head out for a change of water.

Almost to the room door, Mistress stopped her. "This ain't all there is, you know."

"What's that you say?" Sylvia propped the basin against her hip and held the pitcher at her side.

"I may not have come from the most rich side of life before I became the wife of Early Purvis, Silva, but I have experienced real living before." She fumbled with the stitching on the blanket. "But I know you don't know a thing in the world about living."

Sylvia shifted her weight.

"Don't you want to know?" Mistress said, yawning.

"Course I do, Mistress, but this the life the good Lord gave me, so I'm gon' call it mine and do with it the best I can."

"Oh stop it!" Mistress waved her hand in the air. "You are a free woman! This life you are doing the best you can with hardly adds up to living." She was sitting up in bed now, wide awake. "Don't you ever want to leave this place?"

"I'm fine, ma'am." And even if she weren't, Sylvia really wasn't in the mood for fantasies and unrealistic optimism.

"But times have changed! You can be more than fine now. You can be anything you want to be." Mistress looked towards the open window as though it called her by name. "And you can be finer away from here."

Nothing but a quiet bit of morning breeze passed between them.

Sylvia rubbed at her tired eyes with the back of the hand holding the pitcher. Even though just outside the window, spring pollen was turning everything yellow, she felt winter deep inside her. "Ain't much adventure left in me, Mistress. Guess I'll have to stay here and die with you."

Mistress smiled. "Let me tell you this: if I've got to continue on with life here after you die, it sure would make me feel good to know that you lived some point of your life free."

"According to the law and to nature, Mistress, I already am."

"And according to the knot you've been trying to hide under that headscarf, you aren't..."

While Mistress babbled on about so-called freedom, Sylvia kept her ears open for any sounds coming from across the hall, where Mrs. Purvis was awake and perhaps, complaining about Negroes starving her to death.

"...so this is the time, Silva, to—"

"Pardon me, Mistress, but I really need to get started on my day. No tellin' how far along Nan and Dollet are with breakfast, and I don't want you or Mrs. Purvis to wait on your food." When she saw

Mistress' eyes well up, Sylvia added, "We gon' finish talkin' 'bout this freedom later on. We will." As much as she was ready to get out of that talk, she prayed a prayer of thanks for Mistress waking up in much better condition than she did after her last spell.

Sylvia's feet stomped into the walking path trying to keep up with the girl. She was tired and panted in the night air stirring over Butler thinking why in the world had she let Dollet drag her 'cross the river about some meeting she did not care about. She had work to do at home. There was no telling what condition Julius would be coming home in and she wanted to have a little time with her garden. She needed time to just be, run free from all the thoughts running amok in her head.

But she did not want to disappoint the girl. Dollet wanted her to meet her man. It had been almost six months since the two love birds jumped the broom, a non-sense gesture Sylvia did not find the least bit meaningful for any wedding. Black folk, white or green folk. Why would she or anybody else want to jump over a broom, something that stood for pushing dirt around? It made no sense like a million other things people did. If she had known then what years of sweeping up broken pieces of married life had taught her, she would have picked up a broom and knocked herself across the head.

Dollet was in love. Twinkles stayed in her eyes and kept her fitting in with the many stars hanging above them. This was the day, the one day a week she would get to see her man, her Bucky. Though she was a short-framed girl, her strut was long and destined. She could not get to Chewy's fast enough to see if he had made it there from the other side of Mercy where he had found good work.

The night was a secret meeting night for Lions. They were making plans to leave in larger packs. It was safer. Or not. Either way, they needed to plan and Chewy's was as good of a gathering place as any.

The first time she'd heard about it, Hartha Gables, Julius rushed up the path looking a sight. He almost fell over coming up the two steps that lifted their cabin from the ground saving the floor from the rain. She could hear him stumbling outside the screen door and held back her laugh. The last thing she wanted was to change his mood from whatever had him all worked up and in such a hurry. "SookSook!" He called her by the name when something good was happening in his favor. Other times, he said it when the part of drunkenness that makes a man smile like an old chessy cat from ear to ear took a hold of him.

"Yes Junebug." Sylvia played along with his excitement. His mood was contagious. Even she had a smile on her face sitting in the old chair mending a few pairs of old socks once belonging to Master Purvis. Mistress had been fed up with the constant holes in what she called poor material. She told Sylvia to toss them out, but instead, Sylvia stuffed them in her apron pocket to take home to her own husband who was in bad need of them.

"What you doing?" Julius sang the words, leaning over to kiss his wife on her damp forehead. Not much breeze stirred through the open window and everything seemed hotter and more sticky than usual. That kind of kiss from that kind of man was rare, but Sylvia took it. She took what she could get, whatever he gave her to build up the reminders in her

head of his love for her. She took it and held on tight. Until he knocked it out of her later, it was hers to hold.

"Mending you some socks, man." They both laughed.

She missed the sound of Julius' laugh. It had gotten lost in his growl. Sylvia held on to the moment, readjusting the string of thread a little tighter around her finger.

"You hear 'bout that new city, Hartha Gables? Sound like a paradise." His eyes were glossed over talking up into the roof. "Piccolo tell me Black folk got houses big as White folk over there. And they own they own land and mules and they own tools. Don't nobody work for nobody, Sook. Don't nobody own nobody." Julius stared off into the roof and then out the window. He looked as though he could see all the way to Hartha Gable straight past Mistress' old curtain flapping in the bit of breeze finally stirring. Julius was drunk on a dream and Sylvia knew better than to say a word to wake him up.

She tore the end of the thread with her tooth and knotted it. She grabbed the next sock and struggled to figure the best way to put the gaping hole in it back together. "You hear what I tell you?" Julius questioned, irritated.

"I sure do."

"Ain't you excited?"

She wanted to ask him what about it he expected her to be excited about? Why should she be excited about some fantasy town she did not live in? Her life was on Purvis plantation. Sylvia had not been born in Mercy, but for sure she knew she would end up buried over on Butler with everybody else, whole and pieced together. "I see you is." She avoided her honest answer.

"*You bet your sweet head I am.*" *Pulling the thread through the stitch, she looked up at him with stretched eyes. She could not remember the last time Julius let the word "sweet' come out of his mouth except when he was talking about a potato.* "*We gone go.*"

"*We gone what?*"

"*We gone go to Hartha Gables.*" *Julius poked his chest out like he was declaring some kind of big business.* "*You and me leaving this White-pepper town and we gone go over to Hartha Gables.*"

He was serious. Sylvia secured the needle through the sock and sat it on her lap. Her fingers laced themselves between each other and settled on her stomach with her elbows resting on the sides of the chair. "*Oh no. Uh ah. Don't you look at me like that Sylvia,*" *he said. She was no longer his Sook. She stiffened and clenched her teeth tight.* "*We gone get out of here and go where we belong.*"

Not wanting to lie to him Sylvia didn't respond.

"*Listen here.*" *Julius' eye began to twitch while his feet took a step closer to the chair where Sylvia sat. She sat as straight as her back would let her and braced herself.* "*I ain't in love with these people like you is. Mercy ain't where I wanna be. So you better hear me when I tell you we leaving here just as soon as I can get things right. You got that?*" *He did not wait for her response. He had said what he said and that was that.*

Sylvia thought about all the better things she had to do with her time than rush over to Chewy's to listen to senseless talk about a Black folk paradise. If it weren't for the tender spot she held for Dollet, she would have blown the begging and pleading off days ago when Dollet first asked her to go. But she was here now, making her way through a screen door with a hole so big, the screen may just as well not have been there. It did nothing to keep out the flies swarming around the smell of overcooked pig feet and cornmeal mash. For sure, it did not hold in the tobacco smoke, creating a hazy welcome, inside the place and out.

"Come on in." Chewy's wife smiled big at the two women, handing over two jars of room temperature water. A bone-tired Sylvia sipped the drink before she could find a seat at the table with Dollet and another woman wearing a headscarf similar to her own.

The crowd was thin, a few people here and there, with more entering in the place. A stout man blew smoke from his pipe across the cluster of heads, deciding where to sit. He pulled out a chair at an empty table. Two men playing banjos sat on milking pail and a flipped-over pot much like the one she had at the cookhouse. Behind them was Julius' friend, Piccolo, blowing away his troubles through the tiny windows of his harmonica.

Somewhere between the tunes and her sips of water, worry made its way through all the activity going on around her. What if they got caught? What if the White folks figured out this place was not just for drinking and eating? Which one of them would they pick to hang first? Sylvia wondered.

"You want something to eat?" Chewy's wife twisted her wide hips between the tight tables. Sylvia and Dollet both shook their heads. "Something to drink?"

"This lady here'll have a glass of that good stuff from the back." He winked and Sylvia felt his rough, heavy hand on her shoulder.

Julius.

She had known there would be a good chance she would find him there. Chewy's was more home to Julius than their cabin. It was his drinking spot and there was no way he would miss being in the company of people wanting to talk about his same enthusiasm of heading off to Hartha Gables. The place kept him up on his sober nights, dreaming with his eyes open. He would sit on the porch twirling a twig between his fingers and be miles away from the sound of Sylvia's voice telling him to come inside before the mosquitoes made a meal of him.

She did not drink. Never in all her years had she tasted any liquor of any kind. She had no desire too. Between the effect she watched it have on Julius and the way the taste of the drink could swing Master Purvis from a bad man to a worse man, she knew better than to fall under its spell. Julius knew how she felt about drinking. She never liked it for him and she sure did not want it for herself.

She knew better than to refuse the drink. What it could do to her was nothing compared to what years of being at Julius' hand taught her he could do.

The smile painted across his lips was too big for his face and hung off the corners. He had taken her being at Chewy's for the meeting to mean she was coming around on the idea of leaving Mercy. This excited him past his senses. "Only the best for my Sook." Wide smile and pinched eyed over high riding cheeks, he was past excited to see her there ready to make a move away from Mercy.

But she wasn't.

Sylvia was content with the life she lived on Purvis, in Mercy, and was not the least bit thirsty for change. Being free was enough for her. There was still some getting used to that in day to day living. Besides, the danger of being a Lion did not seemed worth the fuss. Being free and living out her days required not a secret meeting and was less likely to end up in a burial ceremony. It just was not worth anybody spilling off scripture over pieces of her.

Julius pulled up a half-wobbling chair for himself from the next table and sat with a nod to Dollet. She smiled big.

"My Bucky'll be here shortly. You'll like him. He's a good man." Dollet blushed, spilling the words all over herself. Sylvia smiled. For a moment, she remembered how nice it was to be young and in love. To be blind and deaf to the years ahead seemed blissful. Sylvia missed it. She looked over at Julius, who was finishing the last gulps of a drink. Her smile faded.

Chewy's wife bought over the small glass of liquor and placed it in front of Sylvia before floating across the room to the next table with the stink of pig feet whirling around her. Sylvia pulled at the scarf around her arms as though the drink had been delivered with a late evening chill.

"Gone on." Julius coaxed. "Drink it."

Sylvia laced her words with a smile at him. "Julius. Honey, you know I don't drink."

"Go on."

She slid the drink over in front of him. "Here, why don't you enjoy it for me." At least she knew what to expect if the liquor went into his body. She knew there would be several more drinks to chase the first one through his system. He would get loud after about one more. Then his words would stumble all over each other in his mouth and fall out covered in spit. Julius would get feisty and pick a fight with the nearest person who would stand still long enough for him to take an unstable swing at them. He would cuss. And then he would sleep. She did not want to know what such a thing would do to her.

With the way it smelled on the nights he came home with it reeking from his pores, she was sure the taste was awful.

He slid it back to Sylvia. "No. I said you go on and drink it. Try it." His voice was getting firm. Sylvia's spine tensed as she saw Dollet watching her out the corner of her eye.

A moment passed and neither of the three said a word. Sylvia tried again. "Julius. Junebug. I don't really want to drink this. Besides, my stomach's been flip flopping all day."

"Then this here just what you need." He slid the glass closer to her. "It'll fix you right up." Julius kept his eyes on Sylvia. Waiting. Dollet tried to look away and keep her eyes glued to the front door where she was waiting for Bucky to come in.

The few candles lighting the secret meeting created a backdrop for the huge shadows growing around Sylvia. Her heart quickened as she wrapped her hand around the full glass. Julius' eyes poked holes of fear in her that would turn to anger if she did not drink up and quickly.

"Go on." He said.

She took a sip. It tasted like a bad combination of herbs boiling her mouth. Her chest burned and she could feel the heat dropping into her stomach. For a moment, it did not settle well and she worried it would come back up.

"See!" Julius slapped the table, excited. "That's good stuff, right?"

She kept silent and avoided looking at either of them, especially the girl beside her. Sylvia was sure Dollet could feel both her tension and her fear. The liquid laid against her stomach. Sylvia offered Julius a slight smile to keep the peace.

"Drink some more."

"Julius, how about you finish it up for me. I'm not really that thirsty."

His eyes narrowed.

Her heart quickened.

"Drink it."

"Julius."

"Goddammit woman, drink it! I'm paying good money for you to have a good time here tonight. Drink the drink and don't you waste my hard earned money." He slapped the table again, this time startling Dollet. The poor girl's eyes stretched in horror. This was what she would have to look forward to. "Drink it and you better drink it all!"

Sylvia turned the glass to her head again, the liquor shaking in her hand. With a deep breath, she poured more of it down the back of her throat. With half the glass emptied, she put it down to take a breath. Breathing so heavy, her own chest and Dollet's matched in rapid rhythm.

"Drink it!" Julius yelled again.

"Bucky!" Dollet jumped from her chair at the sight of her man walking through the door. He had arrived right at the moment to save her from the madness she had ended up in the midst of. She rushed away from the table, away from the future Sylvia was sure all wives would endure. She turned for a moment to see the young couple, Dollet safe in Bucky's embrace. Julius reached for her wrist, still holding the glass against the table. Without thinking, or maybe with, she snatched away.

Julius' nostrils flared but he said nothing, searching her face.

Sylvia, a different woman than the one even she knew, stared back at him with intensity. She wrapped her fingers tight around the glass and with wide eyes beaming into her husband, drank down the rest of the bronze drink and slammed the glass to the table. She pressed the gulps down her throat with a hard swallow, her eyes still on him. When the liquor had made its way into her belly, she stood from the table and peered down at him.

It was the first and the last time she took a drink. It was awful. But so were the moments of fury Julius had laid across her back when she did not obey him or make him happy by having her own thoughts. That night, though, he exposed their damaged marriage beyond the walls of their cabin and it hurt worse than any beating.

"Your money's worth."

Sylvia spit the words at Julius and walked away from the table, past Dollet and Bucky. Past Chewy's wife. Past the music crooning out her pains near the door. Down the stairs, she passed Lions heading inside the joint. She passed her own worry and did not think of what Julius would do to her when he got home. Sylvia just kept going, headed to where she should have been in the first place, to rest up for tomorrow's work of packing up Mrs. Purvis and sending her on her way - another lash for her to endure.

chapter 6

"You're dead to me, girl. You hear me? Dead!"

The rain washed and restored the pure hatred, and pain on Ida's wrinkled face. Both their tears mixed with the water from above and the thunder rolled across the sky. It reminded them of the hearts pounding against the old woman's heaving chest and the one in Nella Jo's young, small framed body with the roundest stomach in front.

"I pray you sow a seed jus' like yo'self in that baby! And when you do," she shook her head with closed eyes, *"Lord have mercy on you when you do."*

For years, the words never left her mind. Nella Jo listened to the thunder roll across the floor of the sky and drew the covers tight around her neck. She tossed and flipped herself from left to right, on top of the covers and now back beneath them for a third time. She was too warm. The memory of her mother's words long ago burned at her mind and skin. They had been the beginning of her motherless life. It was Nella Jo who delivered the order from Master Butler for Ida to live out her days tucked away in a cabin at the back of the quarters. Ida had been the one in Nella Jo's ear screaming and yelling what was wrong and more wrong about the ways Master Butler had begun grooming her to be his mistress.

Nella Jo, young and naive, had slept in the arms of Master Butler while his wife was pregnant and unable to take him in for the discomfort. The day she pushed the baby out, she died and so did the boy. A baby stirred in the cramped space of Nella Jo's womb, stretching and growing her way into her father's heart. The baby came at a time when Grayson Butler's heart laid low on the ground in mourning for the child he never held or heard wail in a hungry cry. Yuna slid from her mother in the morning hours, Master Butler perched outside her cabin. When the midwife had tried to place her baby Yuna on her chest, Nella Jo refused the child and pointed to the door, panting and drained. Yuna had been for him. She was the prize his now dead wife had failed at giving him and Nella Jo was proud of herself as she smiled into the night and drifting into an exhausted sleep.

The child had a mind of her own and her father's heart. If Nella Jo told Yuna to go high, she would go low. If ordered to go right, indeed, Yuna would take off in a full sprint to the left. Disgusted with the child before her fourth birthday, Nella Jo complained to no one, especially her dear Grayson, who believed the child could do no wrong. To him, Yuna was the darling image of a strong-minded girl who would take his reigns one day and carry his name. He did not want for another child, or even a son. Yuna had every crevice of her father's heart and for that, he showered her with a returned love.

In time, Nella Jo's role in his life, as mother of his child grew into more. More and more often, he would have her dismiss the house staff at night so that it was only the three of them. Many nights, he made his way downstairs to the small room beneath the kitchen to lay with her. Though still, it was in the morning Nella Jo would always find him peeking in on his sleeping daughter just to admire her beauty.

When Yuna came of age, in her mid teen years, educated and adored by the people of Butler for her gentle and helpful presence, Nella Jo became infuriated her daughter did not have more of a ruling hand over those beneath her and worse, she had no desire to. She was the Butler heir who mingled and worked amongst the servants. It was not proper and caused Nella Jo constant anger. Even more, the more Yuna connected with the slaves, the less she cared for the presence of her mother. She spent her spare days with her grandmother in the cabin or by the river scribbling away or in some senseless activity with the servants. It was a disgrace and kept Nella Jo up many nights, like tonight.

The rain thrashed against the window, startling and exciting her at once. Adjusting the covers again, she thought of Yuna off in her cabin down in the quarters with the others, refusing to say a single word to her mother at the dinner they shared in the kitchen. She had a way of pouting which drove Nella Jo crazy. The way she would, on purpose, use the wrong fork to pick at her food and eat. Yuna knew it irritated her mother when she clanked her tea cup against the saucer, so she did in excess at dinner. Even more, she refused to indulge Nella Jo in conversation about why the chicks were so important.

"For goodness sake, Yuna there'll be more by morning!"

By the time dinner was finished, the storm started outside with brisk winds. Yuna pulled the shutters closed in the parlor and headed out, in the midst of an approaching storm, glad to have a reason to leave sooner than later from her mother's presence.

"This is precisely what I'm talking about Yuna!" Nella Jo called out behind her silent daughter, still refusing to talk to her as she wrapped the maroon scarf, a gift from her father, over her head and around her shoulders. "We have servants for that sort of thing. And you simply must come to terms with the reality that you are not one of them." Still the girl said nothing. The next sound Nella Jo heard was the slam of the kitchen door just as a wind carried shaken leaves and slight raises of sand across the path. Yuna was gone.

In her own room, Nella Jo gave up on sleep and rose to the side of the bed. A small desk near the window held the last letter she'd gotten from Grayson two weeks ago. He'd been vague of his whereabouts. Most times when he left he offered no detail of where he was going or when he would return. A kiss to her forehead and an *"I'll return. In the meantime, take care of things as I would,"* was all he left her with and it was enough, for she loved the power and control it gave her.

It was nights like this she found herself sleepless and would creep up the stairwell with no candle for sight and slip into Grayson's bedroom. His pillow still carried the scent of cologne. Nella Jo inhaled every bit of the three and a half months Grayson had been gone. More than ever, she craved all that was forbidden to her. In his bedroom, she climbed into his oversized bed as she had many times before, with only the moonlight and rising sun to witness. Beneath the covers, Nella Jo removed her night slip allowing the sheets to caress her body as he would. She was no longer the young girl waiting timid in her room where Master Butler would come down to lay and hold her small breasts. She was a woman. She was his First Lady.

In her own hands, her breasts felt smaller, yet still firm with erect nipples, resting against her upper stomach. Nella Jo dared touch them in the way his massive hands would. With her eyes closed, she imagined the brush of his unshaven face against the back of her neck, his kisses on her shoulder. She was his, then and always. Her own hands explored her body in all the places he once touched, the home she knew in her heart he hungered to return to. When her own body released her longing for him in the rapid movement of her hand, the jerking of her own hips, and then in repeated shivers, she cried. The downpour of her late night longing dampened her thighs as she turned on her side in a fetal position. In the morning, she would order the sheets to be washed again for the second time this week. She had instructed the house servants to keep his room ready at all times for his return, which meant continuing to wash his sheets each week, as if he were still here. She would order the bed to be remade with each corner pulled and tucked tight the way Grayson preferred. But tonight, as the storm roared outside the window, she gathered the sheets in her arms and adjusted his pillow beside her body as a placeholder of the way he would lay, relieved and drained. Nella Jo laid with tears in her eyes until finally, the sleep she craved came.

The sound of hooves. A blazing sun. The bedroom window.

Nella Jo awoke, nearly blind, scrabbling from the sheets and found her night slip.

"Dear God, who on earth could be outside? What time is it?" She mumbled tossing the sheets everywhere.

She was a sight in her night slip and robe half on, slipping down two of the stairs.

Before Nella Jo could fully compose herself, she was met with the eyes of a boy, black as night. At first the boy smiled, with two missing front teeth, until she narrowed her eyes his way. He knew better and wiped the smile from his face quickly. She glared at him in such a way he lowered his head and continued carrying in a trunk. The curved top meant someone of wealth was about, though she was not expecting anyone.

Pulling herself together, she walked down a few more stairs.

And then he walked in the door. Her dear Grayson. Nella Jo exhaled and clutched at the robe and her leaping heart. She wanted to run to him and stand still to savor his presence all at the same time.

Grayson did not notice her on the stairs.

She was grateful, remembering and embarrassed by her attire. Still, she wanted to spring from the remaining stairs into his arms. Nella Jo wanted and wanted, yet resisted. Proper manners were in order.

Grayson passed the staircase.

She waited, then hurried down when he had disappeared, hoping to make it to her room to dress more suitable for his return. Just as she made it to the bottom of the stairs, a woman's boot stepped on her bare foot. Nella Jo ran head-on into the woman, both of them almost falling to the floor. Before she could look to see who the woman was, she was distracted by Grayson's hurried footsteps back in her direction. In an instant, pale white skin and brunette hair, was all Nella Jo had time to make note of before she turned to melt under the gaze she had been waiting for for what seemed an eternity. She had forgotten what she was wearing, the time of day-no one was there but the two of them, her dear, handsome Grayson and she.

Grayson surveyed her in the same manner he would an acre of barren land. Then, at last, a smile crawled over his face. It was the smile Nella Jo had longed to see, the one she imagined he wore in the letters he wrote.

Beyond all law, his smile was her emancipation.

"Oh, my darling," Nella Jo heard him say in a voice sending shivers, again, through her body. Blushing, she looked down at her bare feet, hiding her glee. "Are you alright?"

"Why, yes, dear Grayson," said an echo of Nella Jo's own voice from behind her.

He stepped closer, past her and to a White woman with big curls wearing a dress with more flare than any she had ever owned. Her arms and hands were gloved, and beads of sweat formed on her smooth forehead, which she patted with a cotton handkerchief bearing the initials G.B. for Grayson Butler.

Grayson brushed past her, through her, to the doll-faced woman's side, taking her by the arms and ushering her into the dining room. For only a moment, he paused to look back as if seeing Nella Jo for the first time, a disgust of a black woman wearing a nightgown in mid-afternoon.

"Nella Jo," he spat. "Make yourself useful and bring us both cool waters. It was quite the hot and exhausting ride in for Mrs. Butler. And for God's sake, put some clothes on. You look absolutely ridiculous."

chapter 7

MISTRESS HELD A TREMBLING HAND to her temple as she walked out of the bedroom with Sylvia at her side. Her head was still hurting, but she insisted on getting up and joining Master Purvis and her mother-in-law for late breakfast. Mrs. Purvis was leaving and Mistress felt a slight bit of guilt for being cooped up in her bedroom since the night of the nasty spell at the party.

"Be sure and hold on to that banister, Mistress. Maybe I should walk beside you."

"Oh please stop your fuss, Silva. I can make do just fine."

"Well, just gotta take your time. Food still be on the table waiting when you get to it."

The two made their way down the stairs, Mistress holding on to the banister and Sylvia right behind her. The dizziness was just as bad as the throbbing. From the dining room, they could already hear the driving pitch of Mrs. Purvis' voice. She spoke without pauses, which was fine since Early was a man of few words especially in the presence of his long-winded mother. It did not matter how close it was to the noon hour, it was still too early to deal with the woman's yapping. Mistress stepped down from the last stair and Sylvia rushed around her, reaching for her arm to steady her. She pulled away, determined to convince Sylvia she was fine. Sylvia took her cue and left her to walk ahead on her own. As Mistress approached the dining room door, Sylvia restrained herself when she stopped to take a deep breath, readying herself to go in adorned with a posted smile and livened eyes.

"And if you don't, Son, you mark my words, that wife of yours will be the death of this family's good name."

Mistress stopped just before walking into the dining and took a step backward, hiding herself behind a wall bearing a portrait of her and Master Purvis when they were first married. This time, Sylvia's feet were in motion before her mind could tell her to let her Mistress be. She was at her side, "What's the matter? You feel another spell?"

"Shhh." Mistress held a fleshy finger to her blush, rose lips.

They listened.

A coffee cup clanked against its saucer. "You know that kind of illness runs in the blood."

"Mother."

"Well, it does."

"So tell me, are you a doctor, now?" They listened from outside the door as Master Purvis challenged his mother's fabricated theories.

"Of course not. But I know many people. And several of them are indeed doctors. Blood has a way of carrying what they call genetics from one family member to another. It only makes sense with Vivian and these spells. Just look at her sister. The whole family is a diseased disgrace you've associated us all with."

"How exactly does one relate to the other, Mother?"

They heard the disinterest in his voice. His mother had a way of going on about anything she felt she knew the slightest bit about. The rise and fall of her voice broadcasted how enthralled she was in her own words, in the sound of her voice, she entertained herself. One only needed to give her a nod and a question to show the slightest interest and she would go on until night fell and morning came again if permitted.

"It's all in the blood, Son." The faint sound of toasted bread being bitten into made its way into the conversation. With the pause, they knew it was Mrs. Purvis eating. "When two people, as strange as the parents of those two girls, make children, there's bound to be ramifications like what we have to deal with now."

"And what is it that *we* are dealing with?"

"For Heaven's sake, are you even listening? What I'm trying to tell you is that that wife of yours is mad!" A grunt. "A mad woman bearing our fine Purvis name."

"She's hardly mad. Vivian simply has...illness. These types of things are common, I suppose."

"Common! Common is an unruly bit of skin that needs a good scratching. What she has is the start of the same sick mind as that coo-coo of a sister our good money is paying to keep down at The Sanctuary." Another bite of toast. "Something must to be done, Early."

Sylvia looked up from the floor where she had locked her eyes as they eavesdropped. Her dear Mistress held tears on the rim of her lids. She searched herself for comforting words to say, but rubbed Mistress' back instead.

They could tell by the creaking of the wooden floor beneath his chair, Master Purvis had shifted his erect posture, more than likely from his bad back rather than discomfort of his mother's insinuations. He was not the type of man to stand up for his wife. He left her to fight her own battles against the world, including the ones with him. They continued to listen.

"With all the attention and thought you've put into this Mother, surely, you have a recommendation. So, out with it. Let's hear it."

"Well, it's quite simple. The Sanctuary."

"The Sanctuary?"

"Yes, The Sanctuary. That's where Vivian needs to be sent." Mrs. Purvis sounded pleased with herself. "It's only a matter of time before she reaches the same level of insanity of that sister of hers and all the other touched ones in there. Why wait? Why should you allow her any more time to drag this family's good name through the mud with all of her 'spells' and such?" Mrs. Purvis paused, sipped coffee and slid the cup and saucer aside. "By God, we need to deal with this before it gets any worse than it already has."

Master Purvis did not say a word. Sylvia watched Mistress' breathing quicken. Wanting to ask her to go back upstairs—rest, not listen anymore—she kept her mouth shut, but her eyes open for any sign that Mistress had had enough of what she was hearing and feeling. But there was no sign. Mistress stood with hope.

Sylvia knew the look all too well. Mistress was praying for the impossible. She prayed Master Purvis would say something in her defense for once. She prayed he would tell his mother the spells did not happen often and she was indeed the one going mad.

Sylvia knew all of this from the way Mistress clutched at her chest, eyes closed. It had been by her own bruised hands, clasped together too many times in impossible prayers, she had wiped away Mistress' tears with a clean cloth.

Mistress still believed Master Purvis would turn into a man who would stand up for her and demand the nonsense from his mother stop in an instant. At best, he would at least laugh and dismiss her mother's absurdity before heading out to his horses.

"You may be right." He said.

Sylvia and Mistress both gasped.

She needed him to choose her, just this once, if never at any other moment. Now! She needed him to be her husband instead of being his overbearing mother's son. Her heart sank.

"Mayor Golden's wife told me about a woman once in a similar way as our Vivian. Before anyone knew it, the lunatic woman was walking in the street stark naked mumbling scriptures at all hours of the night. Oh Early, just think of the ruins that would be for us. How would we ever recover?"

"I am still making excuses for the other night."

"And you'll continue to be forced to live lies and deceit on account of her for as long as she keeps up those kinds of shenanigans."

The dining room went silent again.

With her world spinning, inside and outside of her head, Sylvia watched Mistress press her back against the wall with her palms flat against the floral wallpaper. She could read her thoughts in the downward curve of her lips, obvious and distressed. How could this be happening? What was she to do? As if her relationship with her husband was not already strained, here was his mother and her exaggerations murdering what little leverage she had.

Sylvia placed her hand on Mistress' shoulder, her lips drawn. For a moment, she remembered Mrs. Purvis was due to leave later in the day but by the tears reappearing in Mistresses eyes, she decided later would not offer immediate relief.

"This could all blow over in time. People can only talk about such a thing for so long."

"Or they can speak of it forever and hold the image of that pathetic wife of yours lying out on the parlor floor. It's a shameful humiliation, much like those curtains."

"Mother."

"She is not fit to be your wife, Early. There. I said it."

The tears rolled from Mistress' eyes.

"You've said it many times before."

"And I will keep saying it until you realize I am right. I knew from the day I laid eyes on her, skinny as a cane stalk and without a lick of etiquette, she was not worthy of being a Purvis. Oh, but you just had to marry her. Beauty isn't everything! God only knows what was going through your mind about that one."

"I chose her."

"You chose poorly!" Mrs. Purvis hit the table with her small palm. "I've seen you pick better horses and slaves than the wife you chose to wed."

"I suppose."

"So what are you going to do with her? You know I will be leaving this evening and won't be here to serve as a sound mind for you. So what's your plan?"

"I've hardly had a moment to take this all in, Mother. Just give me a minute. I'm definitely going to do something, I just need time to decide. I have to be careful, for Heaven's sake, Vivian *is* my wife. I can't just throw her in that place and walk away."

"Indeed you can! Especially in light of this latest episode at the party. The timing is perfect. Others saw firsthand how she behaved. People are more likely to not question it after such a night. I say the sooner the better."

"Just wait a moment, Mother."

"Early Purvis! A moment is all it takes for her to turn completely mad and ruin your name and run wild with the Purvis fortune. This wife…," Mrs. Purvis said the word as if it were full of filth and mange. "…is nothing of an asset to you."

Again, they did not hear a sound from Master Purvis. He didn't let on to whether he agreed or disagreed.

Sylvia watched the pain-filled tears run wild from Mistress' eyes now. They streamed down her nose and covered her cheeks, hanging from her chin. She did not bother to wipe a single one, letting them collect on her heaving bosom as she kept her agony silent.

"Has she borne you a single child? If not a son to heir you, a daughter at least? Even Butler has that half bred daughter of his to carry on his name."

"She has not." Master Purvis said, defeated.

"Is she upholding her place in Society with all the other prominent women? I think not. And this house," Sylvia imagined Mrs. Purvis looking around, picking out the many things she deemed out of place or of poor decor. "It's in such bad taste. And Early," She spoke in a whisper too late in the conversation. They could still hear her lowered voice from the other side of the door. "I do believe Vivian is taking up an inappropriate closeness with those servants of yours. I'm positive Sylvia slept in her bedroom the other night. The *entire* night."

"But Vivian was ill mother. Of course the maidservant would sleep in her room to care for her if she's ill. There's no oddity to that."

"A slave is a slave! You've given them perfectly fine cabins to keep in. Who knows the danger of having one in your home all hours of the night. I took care to move my trunk to my door so no one could enter."

"Oh Mother. That was hardly necessary."

Mistress' finger twitched. She could not take hearing another word, or lack of words, coming from the two of them. She walked softly past Sylvia to the front porch. Sylvia followed. Mistress sat in the rocker, holding it steady. She needed to be still and settle into everything she had just heard. The afternoon heat had already started to rise from the flowerbed, now full of lilies Mrs. Purvis had ordered the garden boy to change to her liking. Their intense fragrance was nauseating. For a moment, she closed her eyes and tried hard to will the smell away. It did not work, as she felt her empty stomach turn several flips. The last thing she needed was to vomit all over the porch and give Mrs. Purvis more fuel to her fire of madness.

"You alright, ma'am?" Sylvia asked. "Can I get you a cool drink?"

With the raise of her hand, Mistress stood to go back inside, but just as she reached for the screen door handle, Master Purvis appeared pushing the door towards her. Mrs. Purvis followed behind with her lace fan. He mumbled a morning greeting to Mistress and was down the few stairs before she could respond. Mrs. Purvis floated past the two woman as if they were invisible and took a seat in the rocking chair Mistress just abandoned.

"Vivian, dear", She fanned the hot air and lily smell across the porch, "have your girl bring out some iced tea. Its sweltering out here. A wonder you're still standing upright."

By the time Sylvia came back with the iced tea, Mrs. Purvis was well into her complaining and the lily aroma had Mistress' head spinning like a top. She stood against the railing of the porch as Mrs. Purvis' words floated past her the way the brown butterfly fluttered towards the pasture. She gave it the only smile she could summon but still envy filled her heart as she daydreamed herself away from the conversation, the porch, from Mercy. She'd give anything to make the time rush past for the wagon to come for her mother-in-law. Evening felt a far way off from then.

When it did finally come, they said their poised and guarded goodbyes. "Do take care Vivian, Dear. I claim you will be in a more *fitting* state soon." Sylvia watched the woman share an embrace with her son, barely turning a look to Mistress as she waved goodbye into the setting sun.

She was gone. Mistress was thankful, but Mrs. Purvis had left behind troubles marking her hatred in the house.

Even Sylvia found it unusual for Master Purvis to carry on as much as he did with conversation at dinner. He talked about everything from the weather to the disgust swarming around the town about Chewy's. Master Purvis even complimented Sylvia on the gravy she poured over his mashed potatoes. Mistress did not listen to what he said for she was engrossed in her own thoughts, perhaps recollecting the earlier conversation she heard.

"...over at The Sanctuary." Master Purvis' said.

"What?"

"Your sister? When are you going over to The Sanctuary to see her?" Master Purvis put a fork full of mashed potatoes in his mouth. "With you being ill, it's been a few days. I'm sure she's wondering where you are."

It was unlike him to care anything about Mistress' sister, any worry she might have, or even more, how often Mistress made visits. Everything about him was different and causing both women to feel uneasy.

"I think I'll take Sylvia and go into town tomorrow." Mistress gave a slight look to Sylvia and scooped the last of the sweet butter cream. It was Master Purvis who had smeared the majority of the first dish onto his bread. He was indeed like his mother in many ways. "Were you interested in going?"

"Heaven's no. It was simply a question. No reason for someone like me to be in such a place."

Mistress looked directly at her husband. Without a flinch, she laid her knife and fork against the gold trimmed plate a final time. He did not return the look, preoccupied with the last bites of his supper. It was then Mistress lost all hope and love for him.

Mistress stood up from the table, held her tongue in place, and glued her eyes on the stranger at the table with her. Without a word, she tossed her linen napkin onto the table, walked past Sylvia and headed up the stairs.

By the time the fire roared in the cook house, the outside sky had turned a gloomy shade of bluish gray peeking through low hanging clouds. It made the morning break seem prolonged. Stepping outside, Sylvia headed for a pail of water.

"Lord, have mercy!" She was startled at the sound of Mistress walking towards her carrying a lamp she did not need at the hour.

"I'll be fine."

"Why, yes you will, but that doesn't change a thing about the horrible mess you are right now. It's been three days. I'd think the swelling would've at least gone down by now."

Sylvia turned to the woman, her lips swollen. "Thank you for your kind words, Mistress. And good morning to you too." She continued her walk toward the well, picked up a pail along the way, leaving behind her unkind remarks. When she realized Mistress followed, she let out a deep sigh, stopped, and turned to her. "Is there something I can do for you, Mistress? Breakfast ain't due on the table for another hour and I promise you it's gon' be there."

"Yes. There is something you can do for me. And breakfast is hardly a concern to me this morning." Something in Sylvia's spirit told her Mistress' coming request was going to require more energy than she could spare, so she flipped the pail on its top and sat. Mistress blew the flame from her lamp and looked around, careful of eavesdroppers. "I have a proposition for you. For both of us. I mean for you to do, but for both of us to benefit."

"What is it, Mistress?" Sylvia lacked the energy to be intrigued. She wanted Mistress to get on with whatever it was she had to say so she could get herself cleaned up and ready for the workday ahead.

"Tea."

"Tea?" Sylvia laughed then stopped, reminded of her kneaded lip. "Mistress, you down here in your night coat at this hour to ask me 'bout making you some tea?" With her hand to her lip, she managed to still laugh.

"Why yes. Yes I am." Mistress fidgeted with her collar, placing the lamp to the ground. She came closer to Sylvia, again looking around to make sure there was no one within listening distance. "I want you to find a certain kind of tea."

"Well alright." Sylvia dug the ball of her palms just above her knees and pulled herself up to a standing position. She flipped the pail upright and wrapped her lanky fingers around the handle. "Later on, I'll head into town and pick up whatever you need. Right now, I gotta get this…"

"I'm not talking about just any kind of tea, Silva." Her eyes darted back and forth around her, looking for movement. Expecting it.

Sylvia wondered if Mistress was losing her mind. She prayed not. She needed the early morning time for herself and not to be sorting out Mistress' head and life while she was in the midst of trying to figure out her own. Sylvia watched Mistress gather the bottom of her night coat and take another step closer in her direction.

"*The* tea."

Her hushed tone and secretive request agitated Sylvia. She still did not understand the need to make a tea request such a big and private deal. "Is it something I can get for you at the general store, ma'am?"

"Oh no, and..." she looked around, again, "...it's not for me." She placed her hand flat against her bosom, "It's for Early. I want him to drink it."

"You want him to drink it? Is he sick? He bound up? I already got a tea for that sort of thing. Make my own blend with my herbs. I'll bring some with me in the morning. 'Less he need it quicker...he ain't stuck trying to do his business, is he?"

"No, no, Silva!" Mistress was frustrated. She was two steps from a tantrum and Sylvia could not understand why. "The tea is for..." Her eyes widened and her head tilted forward. Sylvia had no idea what Mistress was doing and took a step back"...for..." She made the gesture again.

"Mistress, please just spit it out. I've got chores to get to."

"Good Lord!" Mistress spoke the loudest she had all morning. "Silva, I need you to find the tea so that we can serve it to him so he'll...so that he will..." She searched the look on Sylvia's face for her to complete her words. After a moment, she gave up. "So, that he will expire!"

"Expire?" Sylvia's brows crinkled inward, a wince of pain. "What you mean expire?"

"Yes, Silva. There I said it. I want you to bring me some of that tea your people make. Kifo." She called out the tea with a certain pride around the word as if she was privileged to know it by name.

"Kifo tea?!" Sylvia shouted a bit louder than she meant to. "Mistress, you know what you asking me fo'? You know what Kifo tea do?"

"Why of course I do." She placed her hand flat against her bosom, again, looking around. "Now you go on and find out from your people where to get that sort of thing and let me know when you have it." She picked up the lamp and started to walk away. Her words were too calm for Sylvia to believe Mistress knew what she was asking for. Sylvia reached for her arm. Mistress looked back, surprised.

"Wait. Just wait a minute. Mistress we ain't done here. You can't give Master Purvis that kind of tea. It will sure enough...?"

She nodded her head in a tilt forward of knowing exactly what the rest of Sylvia's words would be.

"So you want me to find a tea that's gonna kill Master Purvis? Is that what you're asking me to do?"

"Shhh!" Mistress surveyed the area, again. "Well don't just blurt it out for all of tarnation to hear, for God's sake." She exhaled deeply and pulled her forearm from Sylvia's loose grip. "But yes. Yes, that's precisely what I'm telling you to do."

"Asking me to do."

"Asking. Telling. Whatever you want to call it. Now will you do it or not?"

"I say not. I don't want no dead white man blood on my hands!" Sylvia threw her free hand, palm up to the breaking sky. "No ma'am. Besides, what in the world got you thinking this kinda way? You still upset 'bout Mrs. Purvis and Master Purvis talk?"

"Yes I am. And Silva, I've got to do something."

"Well, this ain't it."

"What else is there?"

"I don't know. But I do know the Bible say 'thou shall not kill' and I'm pretty sure that mean don't go round killing your husband."

Mistress looked at Sylvia, desperate. "Listen, I can't wait on the Bible or the Lord any longer. This has to be done. And I need you to help me with it."

Sylvia sighed, "Ma'am, I'll leave you to your reasoning. That's fine by me, but I don't want no parts of it. If what you planning got more for me to do than cooking and cleaning and getting on back down that path to deal with mine, well I…"

"How long you gon' wear that headscarf, Silva? There's nothing pretty about it."

"I beg your pardon?"

"That there." Mistress pointed to the scarf Sylvia had worn, washed, and hung to dry every week for the past two months. Sylvia had beautiful hair. It was jet black, thick and soft as cotton, and she wore it in a single braid down the back of her head adorned with a cowry shell at the end that Ida had given her on the morning she married Julius. No one, including Julius, had seen the braid in months or any portion of her hair. What Mistress had seen, which Sylvia did not know, was the occasional blood stain seeping through various spots of the scarf more often than they once had. Days apart, a new stain, in the back and on the right. Another few days and another stain magically appeared on the left. The bruise on her forehead had lasted longer than any other Mistress had ever seen when Sylvia walked into the dining room hiding beneath the same faded bit of calico material she had gifted her two Christmas seasons ago.

"What is it that you're hiding, Silva? Or shall I say what is it that you think you're hiding? I'm a smart woman. I know what I know about that husband of yours and what he does to you just as much and just as hard as mine does to me."

Sylvia rubbed at the latest bump on her head, still throbbing, still causing the world to tilt and shift at times. She was ashamed, and a bit embarrassed. It was no secret the life she lived at home looked just like the one she cleaned up at the Purvis house. Still she did not feel making Julius and his heavy hand 'expire' was the answer.

"It's just not right, Mistress."

"And what's happening to us...being drawn closer to our own death, waiting and waiting with pure terror and fear in every breath day in and day out, is? I beg to differ. I most certainly do."

Sylvia stared down at her feet and then over to the well she had been headed to before all of this talking of expiring and headscarves and tea came into her already painful and exhausting morning. It, the well, seemed so far away. It felt like the days of her life, peace and joy, were far from her reach. She thought what Mistress proposed would not bring her any closer to either one. If anything, it would create an even more painful stain of sin across her holy heart. She shook the thoughts from her head and returned to the woman standing in front of her.

"Mistress, if you don't mind me asking, where you even get an idea like this? And what you know about the Kifo."

"That's not important, Silva. I have my resources."

"You been reading in those books you get in the mail, haven't you?"

"I said I have resources."

"You have books."

"Oh it doesn't matter, I tell you, Silva!" She took a breath. "What matters is you saying yes to what I'm telling you to..."

"Asking."

"I need you to say yes to what I'm asking you to do." Sylvia could tell the words made her uncomfortable by the way she switched the lamp from one hand to the other. "Silva this is going to be a plan for both of us. We're both going to make good on this."

"How so?"

"Well. I'm going to give you something very, very valuable."

"What's that?"

"My word."

"Your word?" Sylvia bent down to pick up her pail and headed towards the well again. "Thank you, ma'am, but no thank you."

"I'll help you keep your hands clean of this."

Mistress called behind her.

"No thank you."

"And I'll get you both safe and in one piece to that Hartha Gables town with money to get started on a new life. One where he isn't so angry about being stuck here and he'll keep his temper and hands off of you."

Sylvia stopped.

Mistress' words rushed over her like the first wind of the morning she could recall feeling on her bare skin. The arm of her dress had been ripped loose and hung down near her elbow. When she reached to adjust the headscarf, her fingers returned before her eyes stained with her own blood. Sylvia knew she was as free as a White man's word and the fist of her husband kept her bound to his beatings. "Remember your children."

"Don't you bring them into this!" She warned her, emotions running rampant.

"My husband is the reason they're no longer here with you." Mistress paused a moment allowing the truth to sink into Sylvia. "And it's your husband who beat the others to death inside of you."

Just then, Dollet rounded the back of the cookhouse and Sylvia motioned her head for her to see Mistress was present. She came closer and gave a slight bow of acknowledgement to the woman dressed in her night coat, outside with the servants, in the wee hours of morning. She took the pail from Sylvia's hand and headed to the well. Dollet had grown into the daughter, the child, Sylvia had longed for. A tear welled in her eye as she watched the young girl scurry to the well and begin filling the pail. When she looked back, Mistress was already heading towards the main house.

———

Master Purvis sat on the porch, his face hidden behind a puff of smoke from his pipe. The wagon carrying Mistress on the front and Sylvia in the rear pulled away from the Purvis house, then rounded the curve between the trees, alongside the river, past the cabins and out into the rest of Mercy. It was there, where the trees broke open and the air thinned, that marked the leaving of the Purvis Plantation. Before they were even a quarter mile from the cabins, Mistress started speaking to Sylvia.

"So, I'm sure you've decided my idea will work for the benefit of us both. Yes?" Mistress spoke as though she had already made up Sylvia's mind for her. "Well?"

Sylvia hesitated to respond. They were not alone. The wagon driver looked straight at the dirt road ahead towards town.

"I'm still makin' up my mind, Mistress." Sylvia called from the back of the wagon.

Neither of them said anything more for the rest of the ride into town.

Downtown Mercy buzzed beneath parasols shielding white women with chiseled, lifeless faces walking about the streets in pairs. From cloth shops to fresh vegetable stands, they floated about like happy ghosts with too much care for appearance, posture and impression. White men carried on with their own business, in their own way, free of care and the thoughts of what any other man thought of them. They went about, untroubled, in and out of the bank, in and out of the general store, getting shoes shined and being men. And then there were the women like her, with their Mistress, stuck in a world they heard was changing. Sylvia noticed the wagon, the one with the handkerchief she had washed many times. It was tied in a double knot to the side of the flatbed every morning. The old mule looked as tired and worn as the driver, her Julius.

Only twice had she ever seen Julius in town on the few errands Mistress had bought her along for or to visit Mistress' sister at the asylum. Their wagon passed him, he noticed, and looked away. She wondered if he was ashamed of being a black man struggling with the load of bottled spirits from the back of the wagon? Or, was he ashamed she saw him?

Their wagon trotted past and turned on to a road leading up a slight hill putting the sun right on them. Sweat dripped under the white-lace handkerchief Mistress dabbed from her face, and slid down her bosom as the driver pulled up to The Sanctuary. The sign on the front of the building had rotted, the courtyard full of leaves and pieces of fallen trees, rusted chairs and whatever else had been left to fend for itself. With her lips drawn tight, Mistress reached for the hand of the driver as he helped her down from the wagon. Even from outside, the screams of the patients could very well have been Sylvia's own.

At the end of a long hallway, they came to an open door and found Mistress' younger sister sitting near the window. In a pale ray of sunlight, she bit at her fingernails without self-control.

"Sister." Mistress walked over.

Sylvia winced at the grinding of teeth and nails, which she could hear from as far as the door.

Mistress sighed and rubbed her sister's matted blonde hair, from the roots all the way to the thinned out ends. "Looks like her hair is coming along nicely, don't you think Silva? All the way down to her shoulders now."

Sister stared out the window for the rest of their visit.

Sylvia made Sister's bed, though the sheets were stained with soils requiring more lye and washing than any one of the asylum nurses were willing to do. From her brush, the one once belonging to their mother, Sylvia picked even more strands than she had seen on other visits.

The only words Sister muttered were clear. "Where's Mother, Viv? Where's Mother?"

Some visits were harder than others for the two women. There were times Sister would scream with excitement at the sight of Mistress coming through the door, which in her delusional mind was the vision of her mother. Sister would beg to be taken home and spoke of missing her mother cooking hash and bread on her favorite days. Her pleas sent Sylvia fetching for a seat to sit through Mistress' heartbreak. On the long ride back home, Sylvia would still feel the pain deep inside herself, unsure if it belonged to Mistress, Sister, or if it was her own ache for her babies.

"Mother has gone to Heaven," Mistress would whisper.

Mistress' father had beaten their mother to death two nights after Mistress left to marry Master Purvis. Almost a month had gone by before Mistress found out the news by telegram from a cousin. By then, her mother had been buried, their father hauled off to jail, and Sister tossed in the nut house. For almost a year, Sister did not speak a word. When she finally did, it was to blame Mistress for having let everything happen.

Sometimes, when Sister saw Mistress coming into her room, she would throw whatever the closest object she could get her hands on. Once, Mistress caught the butt end of the hairbrush. Those visits were the hardest on she and Sister both, and the ones Mistress hurried to rush through.

So they were both glad Sister simply ignored them.

On the ride home, the wagon tossed about Mistress and Sylvia. At one point, Mistress gave a swat at the driver's shoulder for him to calm the horses. Sylvia sat quiet through the ride, knowing the horses were feeling Mistress' anxiousness, as well.

Back at Purvis, Mistress staggered inside and was halfway up the stairs before Sylvia could make it around the back of the house, through the warming kitchen, and up the hallway.

"Silva, bring up some tea."

"Yes, Ma'am."

She stepped aside as Master Purvis passed her in the hallway, though it was wide enough for them both to pass. He walked straight through the house and out the back door, headed to his horses. He was off to ride Creek, his favorite horse of all, brown, with very present eyes.

Mistress had slipped into her nightgown and settled beneath the bed covers though it was still early evening, by the time Sylvia entered the bright room.

"Draw those curtains!" she barked.

After placing the tea tray on the desk on the other side of the large room, Sylvia took her time pulling the heavy curtains spanning from ceiling to floor. She used time to linger under the setting sun by filling Mistress with chatter.

"I brought your special tea for your head. Figure that's the matter. That ride back was enough to make even my head hurt. But I do say we had a pleasant visit, and did I tell you I found even less hair in Ms. Sister's brush, today? Yes, her hair growin' out nice and long, ain't it? She may've been actin' the fool, looking out that window and all, but I swear to Jesus your sister had a smile on her face the whole time you were there, Mistress."

It was a beautiful sunset, all pinks and purples, and Sylvia was thankful to have seen the last of it, thankful for the moment to think of her sons and prayed they were thinking of her.

She finally drew the curtains, then carried a teacup over to the bedside and waited.

"Ma'am?"

Mistress laid with the covers pulled up to her neck and her eyes closed.

"Mistress."

Sylvia sighed. The teacup went back on the tray.

She was almost at the door when Mistress jerked the covers down and leaned on one elbow.

"How much longer do you think you're going to need, Silva--or shall I ask, how many more times are you going to let that man of yours knock you around the way my husband taught him to before you see the need for us to do what I suggested?"

Sylvia walked back to Mistress' bedside and leaned in close enough to her face for her to know she was serious about all the talk about the Kifo and killing Master Purvis.

"Look, ma'am, I don't feel no good about this. Don't sit right in my soul."

"Silva, the last time Julius knocked you across the floor, how did it feel? In that soul of yours?" Sylvia pulled back as Mistress sat straight up in the bed and swung her pale legs around to hang off the side. She looked Sylvia straight in her eyes. "This is just as much for you as it is for me."

Sylvia stared at the curtains.

"Silva." Mistress stood up, putting her hands on Sylvia's shoulders, tears in her eyes. "If we do this, you stand a good chance of being able to go and find your boys, your babies." The bony finger under Sylvia's chin tugged her face. "And I'll help you any way I can. I will, Silva. That's my promise."

chapter 8

THE GRAYSON BUTLER WHO RETURNED was not the man Nella Jo had come to love in all the years she had lived in the big white house. He had returned with a look in his eyes she had never seen before. His tone, when he spoke to her, carried displeasure. "Have someone prepare the west room," he said with not an ounce of remorse before heading into the dining room. "And be sure to fill it with fresh flowers. The lilies are Mrs. Butler's favorite." He placed his hand on the woman's shoulder.

"Yes, sir."

Nella Jo spoke with a numbness in her spirit. She called for the servants and relayed Master Butler's instructions. When they were done, she took her place as the head servant, but a servant none-the-less, a role she had loved her way in and out of, and checked behind them to ensure everything was fit for the new woman of the house. She headed up the stairs, through the motions of checking the sheets on the bed, making certain the curtains had been opened, and the lilies—the intoxicating aroma of the lilies—filled the west room. When she was done, she dragged herself downstairs and retreated to her room where she rested her palms open on the bedspread and finally cried.

The following days tore through her in a fury. In the past months since Grayson's departure, the number of servants on Butler dwindled. Another group had taken off in the middle of the night for Hartha Gables. The few that returned came back in pieces and were buried down in the back of the cabins in the negro cemetery. Nella Jo had not been a servant of any kind since before she felt the first kick of her child in her stomach and told Grayson of her expecting, and she refused to let the new Mrs. Butler turn her back into one. She had been forced to recruit a few women from the quarters to help with the house chores and meals.

One in particular, Very, was an old woman long past her working days but who knew her way around the kitchen, slow as she was. Very's food pleased Master Butler in his return, a name Nella Jo's tongue was learning to say again. Master Butler. Meanwhile, the new Mrs. Grayson Butler was settling in quite comfortably and had begun to make requests, even minor threats.

"Smoked ham is what I asked for...Why, can't you understand I prefer my curtains only half drawn...A yard of calico from town is in order and some tonic for my stomach, this food is just so full of..." Nella Jo listened to the woman bark at the servants day in and day out. She kept her distance when she could and often pushed other servants the woman's direction when Mrs. Butler called for assistance with some meaningless task.

Nella Jo walked around in a state of fear she had never known, or had stuffed so far back into her memory, it did not belong to her. She questioned Master Butler with her eyes. She still, after all the years, insisted on keeping the responsibility of laying out his clothes and serving his afternoon drink for herself. Did he still love her? Had he forgotten her in the time between his last letter and the day he returned with another woman draped across his arm? Who was this new woman? Where had she come from? And did she know she was the mother of Grayson's child? Did she know that it was she who knew the way her dear Grayson breathed just before he dozed into his dreams? Who the hell was this woman and how had she manipulated his love? What, besides parasols and hair pomades and silk underthings, did she possess that Nella Jo did not?

Very, gray and slow, would walk up from the quarters every morning to help prepare breakfast. Because it took her quite some time to travel, she started off when the moon was still making its way for sunrise. One morning, about a month after she began coming to help, Nella Jo walked into a kitchen where breakfast should have been started—Mrs. Butler's request for flapjacks laced with gold and smoked ham fried in ambrosia—to find Very had not arrived yet. Nella Jo threw her frustration into preparing the breakfast alone and setting the table where Master and Mrs. Butler sat on opposite ends. The woman's laughter over a funny walking piglet made its way into the kitchen where Nella Jo worked, making a bigger mess than any kitchen had ever seen. Annoyed, with no one to blame, she stomped down to the quarters to find out what was keeping the old biddy from her work. It was too quiet, though the workers were already in the fields working. As she got halfway down the hill, she noticed Very sitting under the old whipping tree.

"This sure ain't no way to prepare breakfast on time," Nella Jo said even before she neared her. "I had to do everything myself. Everything! Even looking into the face of that ghost woman."

Very's eyes stayed closed. Nella Jo shook at her shoulder and called her name.

She was dead and fell to her side without a brace for the fall.

Nella Jo sucked at her teeth. "You better be grateful to be dead you old selfish coon, or I would have told you a thing or two about how rude you are for dying on a day when there's laundry to be done."

She headed back up the hill for home, but guilt snuck in and turned her around. She headed down to the quarters to let the necessary people know about the body, then rushed back to the main house to finish morning chores. In the next few days that went by, she yelled a bit louder and found the most cruelest of cruel words to address the servants in her anger.

At night, there was no longer room for pleasures, and she could not remember her head touching the pillow in exhaustion. Then one night, her door opened, and though she was tired, she was easily awakened by the hope of seeing Grayson's moonlit silhouette in the doorframe, of smelling his scent. Sure as day and night, the door closed behind him and her sheets were pulled back. Her breath was trapped between confusion and desire for the man, so she laid and waited on his lead. He'd never knelt beside her bed as he did, his face close to hers. He kissed her. Tenderly, as the mother of his child. Through the kiss, he spoke words only her heart heard. Before she knew it, her nightgown was lost in sheets and Grayson was her covering. His hand stroked the length of her tired spine and cupped her backside. When he entered her, Nella Jo permitted herself to release the confusion and the heartbreak. In his ear, with her arms wrapped around as much of him as she could, she cried out, "I love you my dear Grayson." Her body rocked in rhythm with his as he plowed into her, each stroke tearing away her hurt. When he released, he laid against her and shivered, his face buried in her neck. As she reached for the sheet to cover them, he withdrew, then rose, and closed the door behind him.

Before the sun had fully risen, Nella Jo went out and touched the huge live oak tree that knew her secrets. She delighted in knowing Grayson was still hers and Mrs. Butler was for public show, just for appearances and not for love.

"Oh dear, can't you get anything right," Mrs. Butler scolded one of the servers the morning they had added one too many spoons of sugar to her tea. "I'd think you were trying to kill me if I didn't know any better. Bring me a fresh cup." Mrs. Butler switched the way the flatware had been placed before her. The man whose smell Nella Jo still carried, slid the scrambled eggs onto his fork and shoveled them into his mouth. "My Grayson here provides me with all the sweetness I need." Her giggle filled the room, making Nella Jo move a bit faster in hurry to leave and tend to work anywhere else but within earshot of the woman.

Back inside, the grating sound of Mrs. Butler's voice made Nella Jo twist the rag in her hand as she washed a cup for her own tea. She imagined the woman's neck and her frail body wringing in the grip of her fingers. Just then, a butterfly flew in through the open window and in front of her face. With the rag, she swiped it to the floor and took great pleasure in the crackling under her boot.

That night, Nella Jo leaned against the live oak again and let herself feel the connected fragments of bark on the trunk.

"Nella Jo."

Mrs. Butler, as pale as the dress she wore, came to intrude on her night.

"Yes." She closed her eyes and leaned her head back against the tree.

"My, how informal we're being tonight." She could hear the crunching of leaves as she came closer. She smelled of the soft lilac. "I'd like you to clear the house of everything once belonging to the former Mrs. Butler. For Heaven's sake, it's been twenty years. You should have done this already."

"Nineteen." Nella Jo mumbled.

"I beg your pardon."

"Nothing, Mrs. Butler." She sighed, leaning away from the tree. Looking her squarely in the eye, Nella Jo asked as sweet as pie, "And when would you like to have this done by?"

"Well, I was thinking in a week's time." A lock of curl dangled on her shoulder as she moved her head about surveying the grounds. "That should be enough time for you to rid everything out of my sight that was a part of Grayson's life before me."

"I'll see what I can do." Nella Jo shifted her weight from one foot to the other and returned to the tree. She knew well Mrs. Butler directed her words at her, but refused to let the woman ruin what was left of her night, her time to not be a servant.

"Well, we are done here, then." She heard the woman take steps back towards the house.

Then she remembered.

"Oh, and Mrs. Butler..." she tried not to sound too anxious. "Does Gray...does Master Butler have any special requests, anything he wants to hold onto?"

The ghost of a woman turned back and came a few steps closer. "Nella Jo. Make no mistake, Grayson Butler's requests are being taken care of. Like I said, we are ridding this place of anything that was or thought they were, of importance to him before me. And Dear, if there is anything he needs moving forward, it will be *my* first concern. Whatever he needs you for, will be strictly minimal. It'd be best you come to terms with me being his 'First Lady' from now on."

chapter 9

"So I'll need to bring in a few more workers for the harvest than before. Overseer says this year's going to look pretty lucrative on the books." Master Purvis went on to his wife as Dollet cleared away the main-course dishes and Sylvia spooned peach cobbler onto dessert saucers. She was just serving Master Purvis a spoonful of extra crust when Nan came in from the serving room, her lips pinched together and eyes on the Purvises.

She nudged Sylvia's arm, whispering, "You need to run on over to the cookhouse. Right now!"

"What for? We've already brought everything over…"

Nan stretched her eyes at her friend. "Just go on! Now, Sylvia!"

Her desperate tone had Sylvia nervous all the way across the bumpy path to the cookhouse. She opened the door to the sound of wailing. A little yellow girl turned to her, big tears rolling down her face. It took a minute for Sylvia to see a quiet Julius standing in the corner by the hearth.

"Julius! What on earth you doin' here? And who this baby?" His face looked tired, more than just the regular droop of tawny eyes. Everything in the cookhouse felt heavy as he leaned against the table.

"You alright?" she asked in what was nearly a yell. "What in God's name the matter wit' you?" Sylvia steadied her voice, then walked over and flipped a pail for him. "Sit down, Julius, please."

"Don't wanna."

"Suit yourself. But you look like you gon' fall down if you don't." She rolled her eyes at the stubborn man and walked back over to the other side of the table, where the child stood. She wasn't crying anymore, though her face was beet-colored. "Where you two coming from?" She asked Julius, her eyes on the girl.

"How many questions you gon' ask, woman?" She knew by the sting of his tone to leave him alone. "This here Alivia."

"Alivia, huh?" Sylvia squatted down in front of the girl, who looked to be about four or five years old. Hair ran wild over her head, freed from the satin braid hanging down her back.

"Well, Miss Alivia," Sylvia cooed, "what's the matter that got you all upset?" She sucked in air, the way Sylvia knew a good hard cry tugs on the chest. When she sniffed hard, Sylvia reached up on the table for a clean rag to wipe her nose. There was no fuss from her. "Now you ready to tell me what's wrong?"

"She scared, that's all," Julius said.

"Scared of what?"

The child touched the side of Sylvia's face with the tips of her fingers.

"Don't know what's going on myself, Sylvia. She probably scared 'cause she don't see no mama around. That's why I bring her here to you. She wouldn't stop all that crying. I told her you be home later, but she just kept at it. Couldn't take it no more, so I bring her for you to hush her up."

Sylvia got up. She wondered if this was what her boys lived through, wherever they were now. Had there been some strange woman asking strange questions about them, too? She let out a deep breath. "Where she come from? How she get to our cabin?" Sylvia asked Julius, having to put a hand on her hip to ease the ache off of her back. "Who she belong to?"

Alivia's little hand took a hold of Sylvia's skirt.

"Listen, I ain't come here to answer questions. Bring her home with you when you come." Julius dragged himself towards the door. "I'm gon' get on back so I can get some sleep. Tomorrow be here 'fore I know it."

"Julius!" She called after him. "Julius!"

He headed towards the cabins without so much as a wave of his hand. Sylvia turned back inside to Alivia, who was still latched on to her skirt.

"You gon' have to stay here, hun." Sylvia took her tender hand in hers and led the girl over to the pail seat. "Take this rolling pin." She looked around the kitchen and spotted the big mixing bowl, then sat it in front of Alivia. "Play with these 'til I come right back. And don't you move, you hear me?"

Alivia nodded.

Moments later in the main house, she managed to sneak Dollet, along with a hunk of leftover bread smeared with sweet-cream butter, away from the serving room and back over to the cookhouse.

"Oh she's precious!" Dollet said on first laying eyes on the girl, who was still sitting in the same place Sylvia had left her, neither rolling pin nor mixing bowl touched.

"You gotta stay over here and watch her for me, Dollet." Sylvia was talking fast. "Me and Nan'll take care of things back at the main house, make sure this chil' don't come out, 'cause if Mistress get wind of her being here all hell gone break loose."

Alivia looked at Sylvia and nothing else.

"Alright." Dollet took Alivia by the hand and walked her over to the table, where they started putting flour in the mixing bowl.

"Dough," Sylvia said to herself, "now why didn't I think of that?"

"Ms Syl," said sweet Dollet, "go on now and get them Purvises off to bed. This chil' here's won't be no trouble like them at all."

Seemed like the night would never end with Sylvia's body working in the main house and her mind over in the cookhouse. Master Purvis stared into his whiskey glass while Sylvia refilled it twice, all the while she kept feeling the little girl's hand on her. The smallness of it stayed with her. Every now and then, Master Purvis would swirl the caramel liquid towards Mistress, who sat across from him doing needlepoint. Sylvia counted each swirl, waiting for him to put down the glass, to put an end to the night.

"Well," he said at last, "it's getting late."

Sylvia turned to Mistress, who'd already placed her needlepoint on the side table and was halfway up the stairs." She could still feel the little girls fingers on her face. "Do you need me to bring you up anything, ma'am?"

With a wave of her hand, Mistress went into her room and closed the door. Grateful, Sylvia rushed off to clear away the last of the dishes with Nan.

In the cookhouse, they found Dollet sitting on the pail with Alivia in her lap, both asleep.

Nan sucked her teeth. "That there gon' be trouble."

Sylvia picked up the child from Dollet's arms and watched the peaceful glow on the child's face. "I'm gon' figure a way around this."

"So where she come from?" Nan put her hand in the crook of her hip.

Sylvia did not know any more than Nan did.

"Um hmm, Sylvia. Well, you better get that right 'fore morning or we all gon be in hot water."

"Why?" Dollet yawned and stretched as she stood up. "What's wrong with having a sweet little girl here?"

"Mistress don't care nothing about no sweet, bitter, salty, or sour child. No kind of child's what she want."

"What you mean?"

"Girl, shush and help me get this flour cleaned up off this table so we can all get home!" Nan threw Dollet a damp rag. "All you need to know is Mistress don't like chi'ren no where 'round here."

Sylvia shifted Alivia in her arms, thankful the child didn't weigh much.

"And Sylvia, head on home and get her tucked in," Nan ordered.

On the walk home, she felt the child tighten her arms around her neck, then loosen as she fell into a slumber. Her mind wandered to the river up ahead and thought about the four children she had birthed but had not a single one to show as hers.

Inside, Master Purvis had ordered her to wrap her baby in a cloth made of scraps from the loom house. Her tears had soaked the covering as her firstborn slept through it all. His hands were strong, even for a baby only three days old. His fist was hard and she worried he would have the temper of his father. The thought alone stopped her sobbing just long enough to say a quick prayer over his little soul and the soul of the wife he would one day have.

Sylvia had finished wrapping the baby just as Master Purvis walked back into the parlor, led by a haze of smoke from his pipe. "Well is he ready?" Sylvia could not form an answer and simply held the bundle of her heart towards him. "Don't give him to me. Take him out front on the porch to Oliver. Collector be here soon." He stuffed the stem of the pipe back into his mouth and left.

On the porch, Oliver sat with his eyes closed as tight as the baby's she handed over to him—one of them, not ready to see the world ahead of him, the other not wanting to remember the world behind him. Oliver was near eighty-four years old. He had spent his entire life with the Purvis family, originally with Master Purvis' grandfather and then passed down from one Purvis to another. He had been an errand boy and a blacksmith his whole life. He had been a husband, a father, and now a widower with children that had been sold off over the years. There was not much for him to leave behind other than friends and hard memories. Even those, he did not want to see.

Oliver had watched a lifetime of the Collector's wagon come and go from plantation to plantation collecting the elderly and newborn babies to be sold away. Each were examined for two eyes, ten fingers, and ten toes. Their spines were checked for crooks and the skin for any oozing sores of sickness. For every elderly person or child that made it onto the back of the Collector's wagon, Master Purvis was given a few coins for their worth, while sons, daughters, mothers, fathers, and grandparents were driven away and never heard from again. The day the Collector drove away *with Sylvia's firstborn, she ran behind the wagon until she fell to the ground exhausted by the unbearable heat of the sun and a broken heart.*

Almost home, Alivia flopped her head from one side to the other in her sleep. The gesture thumped against Sylvia's soul as a tear slid down her face.

The next morning, Sylvia was already awake long before she needed to be. Outside, the stars still kept in their bed of sky, as did the child she looked over. Quietly, she knelt and settled in beside the girl and watched the rise and fall of the sheet she had laid across her on the floor pallet. Between shallow breaths, Alivia's lips quivered as though she wanted to utter words, answer questions from her dreams. Sylvia wanted to know the story behind the girl that was now hers, for however long, for whatever reason. With a single finger, she raised a strand of hair from the girl's damp forehead and placed it gently against the side of her face. Her hair was silky, from the night's perspiration and a trace of White blood in her. Alivia's skin was smooth, unscarred by beatings and hardship of slavery. Sylvia smiled, knowing the child would not know the things she knew about growing up on Purvis plantation as a black girl child.

"Mama?" Alivia's eyes opened.

"It's me. Sylvia. Remember?"

Alivia rubbed at her eyes.

"Good morning." She tried to keep her voice low and gentle, not to startle the girl or wake Julius.

"Good morning." She yawned.

"Do you wanna get some breakfast in your belly? It's gonna be a big day for us both."

"No." Alivia's eyes had opened, and they were as beautiful as the moon that sat watching them outside the window. "Where my mama?"

"Your mama's fine, baby." Sylvia felt bad about telling a lie, but she did not know the truth. She did not have the answers or a clue where to find them. "I know she wants you to get the sleep washed off that pretty little face of yours and head on over to the cookhouse with me. How 'bout that?"

As the sun took its place, Sylvia held Alivia's hand as they walked to the cookhouse. Inside, Nan did not bother to stop kneading at the big lump of dough long enough to acknowledge either of them as they came through the door.

"Well, good morning to you too, Nan." Sylvia said adjusting the tie on the back of her apron. Pointing over to the same empty pail from the night before, she directed Alivia to take a seat.

Nan kept her eyes glued to the dough.

Sylvia gave a playful wink to the ray of sunshine smiling over at her.

"She gon' be around." Sylvia offered Nan an explanation she did not even know the details of.

"How long?"

"A while." Sylvia grabbed her own share of dough and started punching at it. Over and over she rolled and beat into the dough.

"Mistress sho' ain't gon' be thrilled about that."

"You tell me the last time Mistress been thrilled about much of anything." Looking over at a bored and yawning Alivia, she tore off a small piece of the dough and rolled it in a ball. When it was round and full, she rolled it across the table to her. Alivia giggled at the squishy and sticky feel of the dough, rolling it around and round. Again, Sylvia beat into her portion. "Besides, Mistress ain't got to know, 'least for a while." She looked up from her kneading just in time to catch the tail end of Nan's doubts.

When Nan grabbed for the rolling pin and begin flattening out her dough, Sylvia went for the old tea cup chipped on the handle they had used to cut years worth of biscuits. Returning to the table, she saw Nan watching Alivia with her ball of dough, mimicking Nan in flattening it with her palm.

"Where this here child come from, Sylvia? You figured that out yet?"

Sylvia kept quiet as if she did not hear the question. By the expression on Nan's face, the missing pieces of the story seemed just as wrong to her as they did to Sylvia. They were both clueless.

"Hmph." Nan pursed her lips at how Sylvia rolled her dough. "Too many missing pieces on that tea cup."

By then, a new day had broken.

chapter 10

Nella Jo was four years old when she arrived on the Butler plantation, her hand and wrist locked tight in the palm of her mother's. There were three of them including her brother Julius kicking his way to his freedom from Ida's womb three nights after their arrival. It was fortunate to have been purchased together but as the mother was pregnant and the child only four years old, it worked in their favor. A four year old could die of mere chagrin without her mother. Nella Jo and Julius were both the children of a blacksmith hung from a tree just outside their cabin where Nella Jo had been awakened by the thump of his body hitting the ground. Ida had paced the floor for him all night, her stomach protruding only a little then. She had dozed off in the wee hours when the men hoisted his already lifeless body to dangle in the bitter morning air. It was the start of fall and everything was changing. The trouble Nella Jo had heard her father come home night after night talking loud and nervous to Ida about, it had caught him, hog-tied him at the ankles and hands and slit his throat to drain the last of his spirit out of him.

Water gushed from Ida and the screams followed right after. Everything happened fast. Nella Jo, standing outside the shack they were still coming to know as home, peeped around the side of the door to watch the women tending to her mother's pain-filled cries.

She was a smart girl even then. She knew how to count, she knew most of the alphabet, though she wasn't able to share the knowledge her mother had given to her with others. Ida had already told her she would see blood fall from her privates one day, and when the day came, she would be a woman with all the honors of bearing children. Nella Jo would have an advantage over women who were dried up in the belly. If she did everything right, Ida told her, she could make a decent life for herself and her children. The important thing she needed to do was be sure the right seeds were planted.

Master Grayson Manning Butler caught her eye by the time she saw the first speck of blood on her undergarments at fourteen.

Mistress Butler was a frail woman. When word she was with child spread across the plantation, there was a hushed sadness and shaking of heads. Everyone knew her body barely held her in and just thinking of it trying to hold up for two people perplexed their minds. The morning her water came, she was in her bedroom, yelling for Nella Jo, who could barely hear her as she stood outside in back of the house.

Nella Jo was vomiting.

"Yes, Mistress." She walked into the room, barely stable on her own feet. She wiped her mouth with the bottom of her apron and ran the back of her hand over her forehead to wipe away the sweat. Mistress Butler was already squatting, dress hiked up around her waist and bloomers wrapped round her ankles when Nella Jo walked into her bedroom. The woman looked more like she was supposed to be in the outhouse. Nella Jo saw the stream of thick, mucus-filled blood and knew for sure something was wrong.

"You gotta help me." Mistress Butler panted. Beads of sweat glued her hair to her face. Nella Jo wondered how long the woman had been calling for her?

"I..I'll go get help," was all she could say and took off with Mistress Butler's soul-wrenching screams calling for her to come back. Nella Jo obeyed.

"Ma'am!" Nella Jo said, "I gotta go and get help."

"You gotta help me." The words slid from the constricting spaces that separated each tooth. "YOU! You are the one that has to help me with this."

Fear flew into Nella Jo's body. Mistress Butler looked bad, like she was taking her last breaths.

"Let's get you up in the bed," Nella Jo said, not sure what else to do. She remembered her mother birthing Julius. She remembered the way she had seen her lay flat on her back with her legs pointed to the Heavens. "You'll feel better laying flat."

It took a while for Mistress Butler's knees to unbend. Still, the blood slid down her thighs. Once she was in the bed, Nella Jo fixed the pillows behind her to make it easier for her to push. Before she could get her moved, Mistress Butler let out another scream, this time she laid Master Butler's name across it. Nella Jo's heart stopped for a moment, disturbed by the woman who called her lover's name.

Ida rushed into the room pushing Nella Jo aside.

"Go get Esther, Nella Jo, and tell her Mistress havin' this chil' and she having it right now! And tell her it ain't gon' wait on her, so be quick."

Nella Jo stumbled down the stairs, across the yard to the chicken coop, where Esther stood leaning against the fence feeding the chicks. She relayed Ida's message, word for word. Esther took off across the dirt. Nella Jo, unable to keep up with the woman, followed behind at her own pace.

Esther looked back. "You alright, girl?"

Nella Jo leaned over, hands dug into her knees, raised up enough to wave for the woman to go. As she continued up to the house, she tried to slow her breathing. By the time she was there, the vomit went across the grass in front of her.

After making her way into the kitchen door, she took the stool near the door, allowing the room to complete its spin. Gripping the side of the stool, she no longer heard Mistress Butler's screaming. Maybe the baby was here. Maybe she had proved them all wrong, and her body could really push out a child. She'd already beat all the odds of carrying the baby inside long enough for her belly to poke out.

Maybe she had delivered a boy.

Or a girl, as Master Butler had hoped for.

"We need your help upstairs cleaning up." Ida walked into the kitchen, a serious and busy look about her, barely looking at Nella Jo as she gathered up old rags.

"Yes, ma'am," Nella Jo dared. "Is it a boy or a girl?"

"Boy."

"Master Butler will be pleased."

"No."

"No? Why not?"

"A dead boy."

Nella Jo almost smiled.

"Mistress Butler alright?"

"She as good as can be at a time like this." Ida finally stopped and looked over at her daughter. "Ain't no more children coming out of her."

Nella Jo felt a bit of sadness, when she really thought about what happened. Ida taught her a woman had a special gift in being able to carry a man's child. Mistress Butler had lost her gift, a child today, all hope of ever bearing another. Everything gone all at once. This would break Master Butler's heart when he returned from the Carolinas. For him, she felt a different sadness.

Ida stared at Nella Jo with her knowing. "Don't worry, girl, Master Butler gone be alright. He still got another chance for that daughter he wantin'."

"What do you mean?"

"I mean I ain't no fool...and you ain't, either. I know about that seed he done planted that got you hangin' out back."

"I..."

"I nothing. Don't need no explanation. Besides, ain't none out there a slave girl can give for tryin' to make her own way." She came a step closer, looking Nella Jo in the eye. "Long as she ain't got no shame." She turned and walked back out of the kitchen with the rags. Nella Jo followed.

Months passed like lightening across a sky just before thunder. By the time her dress began to pudge in such a way Nella Jo could no longer arrange her apron to hide it, the whispers covered the Butler plantation right along with the spring pollen. One day, staring out the kitchen window, she played with the same rag she had used earlier to dry them. It wasn't until her mother put down the tea set and rattled the empty porcelain cups that she turned around, startled.

"You okay?"

"I'm fine." Ida refilled the sugar bowl. Then stopped, realizing she'd already served the tea. She began scooping the sugar out of the bowl and back into the canister.

"You don't seem fine, Mother."

"Well, neither do you, staring out that window like it don't need washing."

Nella Jo knew her mother's anger could not possibly be about the windows she, herself, had just washed yesterday. Ida made her way around the kitchen busying herself with tasks.

"Mother..."

"It's Julius, Nella. I saw him leave this morning." *She leaned her back, which had worked way beyond it's days, against the wall. She stood tall, stretching with her hands on her hips and fingers in the small of her back. Without moving her head, she looked around the room and towards the back door, then carried her voice down to a whisper.* *"I seen him turn at the big gate, and then later run back the otha way."* *She made a grunt like she wanted to hit something or someone.* *"That boy runnin' again."*

Julius had already run away twice since Christmas. It angered Ida knowing he would get caught, making trouble for all three of them. She knew the day was soon coming when he would not be so lucky to make it back with breath still left in him after the catchers whipped him. He was thirteen, and the way he was going, he was not going to see fourteen. *"Why he keep doin' this?"* *Ida grunted.* *"This time, for sure, Master Butler gone beat the tar outta him. Probably do it himself this time. 'Member last time. Julius couldn't stand up straight for over a week."*

Nella Jo came closer. She had grown a few inches past her mother, but with the weight of the baby, they both now carried the same stout frame.

"Julius, gotta make his own mistakes," *Nella Jo said.* *"You can't worry yourself sick. Master Butler see you walking around here with pain on your face, he'll soon find that look familiar and start looking for Julius."*

"He gone get caught anyhow."

"*Maybe. Maybe not. But your long face sure is the right way to shorten any head-start he trying to get.*"

Her mother walked past her to start with the tea cups again. "A manchild'll drive his mother into her pine box quicker than a girl child will. That much I know."

She kept her back to Nella Jo, but she could hear the pain and tears in her mother's voice. Her words made Nella Jo think of the child inside her. She prayed every morning, noon and night for it to come out the girl Master Butler wanted. Especially now. Her hand rested on her high belly until she realized her mother was watching.

"*You better pray hard there's a girl kicking 'round in there. A boy gone break your heart just as well as Master Butler's.*"

When Julius had been gone for five days, Ida and Nella Jo both began to breathe easy, hoping he had made it far enough away from the punishment waiting for him at Butler. This had been the longest time passed, until Nella Jo heard Ida rush into the kitchen gasping for breath.

"*They got him.*" *She cupped her hand to her chest, trying her best to keep her heart inside.* "*They done caught Julius and he strung up to the back of Brunson's horse. Two more men with 'em. They headin' up to get Master.*"

"*Oh Lord.*" *Nella pressed her hand against her own child growing high.* "*Lord, Lord, Lord.*"

"*That's all we got now. Nothin' but the Lord gone be able to spare your brother from the wrath he 'bout to come up 'gainst.*" *Ida fiddled at the buttons of her dress.*

"*You've gotta calm your nerves, before…*"

Ida raised her hand to silence Nella.

"Don't say that to me." Her tone was stern. "They fixin' to string my boy up and beat him to death. Don't you tell me to calm myself."

"I didn't mean..."

"Come shush me the day that baby walkin' 'round here puttin' in a good days work or bleedin' on a rag, and you ain't got no hand in its fate. You helpless. You got nothing to save it from what's ever Master Butler got planned for it."

"But this here's Grayson's baby."

Ida gave a devil's laugh that told Nella Jo she was a fool. "Lemme tell you one thing, Nella girl. I don't care how many babies he put in you, you call him Master Butler. Ain't 'nough passion in the world you thinkin' lie between you and a white man to change the fact you a negro girl. Don't go thinkin' you ain't still the muddy dirt White folk track on they boots."

Just then, the kitchen door opened with a fierce swing.

Master Butler. A tall statue with broad shoulders.

Her heart raced out of fear and all other kinds of things.

"Ida, you need to get on out here. Now."

"Yes, Massah."

Without haste, Ida left with Master Butler, careful not to walk too close behind. Nella Jo rushed over to the door as her mother dropped the hem of her dress, careful not to trip when she stepped down from the last step. Before she could follow them, Master Butler turned, looking past the mother to the daughter.

"Stay."

Nella Jo halted like a trained dog. So badly, though, she wanted to run behind them. The last time her brother ran, Master Butler simply left him on the ground after the whipping. Ida went to Julius, walking beside the two slave men who picked him up and carried him back to their cabin, where she dug a rag of turpentine into the horrible gashes in his back. Now, not enough time had passed for Master Butler to have whipped him, so Nella Jo could not understand what was happening. Her baby stirred inside, its foot pressing against the front her stomach.

After a while, one of the children from the quarters rounded the side of the house, calling her name. She leapt from the stairs as quickly as her stomach would let her.

"Momma say run get you," said the boy or girl--she could not tell--between breaths. "Somethin' awful happenin' down in the quarters. Massah and your momma and your brother. Come quick!"

Nella Jo followed as quickly as she could, setting aside Master Butler's orders. Just as she made her way down the hill and into the Quarters, one of the elders grabbed her by the hand, leading her away from the gathered slaves.

Julius was tied to the big whipping tree, his feet bound and his arms hugging the large trunk. Though Nella Jo had seen whippings many times in her years at Butler, she had never seen a slave tied in such a way. To the right of the tree was Ida, on her knees, crying and begging at Master Butler's feet. She rocked back and forth on the ground. Nella Jo started out in a rushing leap towards them, but the overseer, Brunson, grabbed the neck of her dress and pulled her backwards. She screamed as she fell to the ground, landing on her back.

"Don't let her over here," Master Butler ordered, a pointed finger at Nella Jo on the ground. "Keep her out of the way but don't you hurt her."

"I've got her." Brunson shot back, his boot at the side of Nella Jo.

Her heart broke. Her brother was tied to a tree, her mother begging at the feet of the man whose child she held inside. The same man yanked Ida back up to her feet as she continued to beg, plea and tried to get back down on her knees. Finally, Ida gave in and stood. Master Butler, Nella Jo's Grayson, grabbed her mother's hands and in them put the handle of the whip, tightening her fingers around it by balling her hand into his. He looked her straight in the eyes as he did it, a look more intimidating than the act itself.

"Do it!" Master Butler yelled. Still, Ida begged for his mercy. "This boy has got to learn and, apparently, you gone have to be the one to teach him. Now, I said whip him!" His thunder rolled through the quarters and cut through the cries of the crowd, including Nella Jo.

She refused to sob. For every tear daring to escape the prison of her eyes, she took her palm to her face with a fierce swipe and erased it before it could travel her distinct cheekbones.

"Brunson!"

"Yes, sir." Brunson went to Master Butler, only after turning an eye to remind Nella Jo to stay put where she was on the ground.

"I want you to start out and get him good and ready. Then you make sure Ida finish the job."

"Yes, sir." Brunson picked up the whip from the ground where Ida had released it from her shaking hands. He tore into Julius' back with the first lash. Ida, as if being beaten at the same time, fell again to her knees and bawled into her hands. Again, Brunson drew the whip backwards and into Julius' back, wrapping around his body, molded to the tree. And again. And again. And again until Master Butler had to remind him that he was only "getting the whip warmed up."

Master Butler then stood next to Nella Jo, still on the ground. "Give it to her," he ordered Brunson, who yanked Ida to her feet, forcing the whip into her hand. She dropped it. Brunson picked it up and slapped the woman, not with more than half a head of gray tightly knotted hair, *across her creasing face. Again, he placed the whip in her hand. This time, Ida held it. The cries of the crowd flowed in a hum, Ida's pain filling every body and ripping at each soul. They all hurt for both Ida and Julius, whose blood cascaded from the gashes across his back to the ground.*

"Do it now!" Brunson yelled.

"Master Butler, I beg of you..." Nella Jo started.

"Shut up!" He raised the back of his hand, ready to lay it over her face, then stopped just short of remembering her stomach. She had already clutched her head down and wrapped her arms around her belly to protect it. When he did not hit her, she opened her eyes and looked up at him, still staring at her, hand raised.

It was then, she knew the child inside of her would be their saving grace.

Ida held the whip and cried.

Once again, the overseer swung the back of his massive hand across her face, this time almost knocking her to the ground. When Ida caught her balance just before falling, she stood upright and turned to Brunson. She no longer sobbed as Nella Jo and everyone else watched her prepare herself for the death of the woman she was and would no longer be.

"Do it now! Whip some sense into that boy of yours!" Ida gripped the handle with short fingers, while she stared directly into the eyes of Brunson, who stood close enough to share her breath. Just as he raised his hand, Ida let out a scream that made even Brunson back away. And it was in the midst of the scream that she drew her arm back as far as she could, holding her breath along with every mother on the plantation. It wasn't until the whip rested back against the ground that her scream ended.

She froze, her eyes locked on the tree she had been forced to carve into her only son. Ida watched her own strength and will flow red from his open back. She watched any hope of a life of freedom drain from him. In that one moment, she, herself, died inside at the feet of her unconscious boy, no longer his mother.

Weeks later, the baby arrived. Since the beating, Ida worked less and less, slower and slower. Master Butler yelled and scolded the woman who seemed to have aged more in the short time than she had her entire life. Nella Jo had never seen or heard him speak to the elders on the plantation the way he did her mother. Ida's behavior became more and more peculiar. She would put too much salt in the food, serve Master Butler lukewarm coffee in a daze, and once burned a hole clear through his trousers. Frustrated to a point of red-faced anger, Master Butler would order Nella Jo to deal with her mother and make things right. When even she could no longer coax any more work out of Ida than he or Brunson, he would take his frustration out on Nella Jo with yells and an occasional slap in front of others.

Master Butler came to the cabin Nella Jo shared with Ida and Julius for the first time since Yuna was born. Nervousness rushed over her still recovering body. She held the baby wrapped in cloths out to its father, yet, he did not make any gesture to receive her.

He walked the length of the small cabin, surveying the walls and the single chair. "Are you comfortable here?"

"Yes, sir. We make do."

Master Butler grunted as she walked over to the pot of dinner Ida had left before heading to the river to sit and hum into the night as she often did since the beating. He stuck his finger into the warm soupy mush. "Dammit! Did that mother of yours cook this?"

"Yes, sir, she did."

"That's what I thought." He wiped his hand on the side of his pants. "It's not fit for anybody's eating with that much salt." Without another word, and the same furious look he held on his face whenever he encountered Ida, he left.

The next week, Master Butler moved Nella Jo and his baby to the small room outside of the kitchen inside the main house. She had shared a cramped cabin with Ida and Julius since she was a child, so it was only natural she felt a bit of sadness being away from her family and living new roles. It took time to adjust. She was a new mother, a nighttime companion for Master Butler, and now in Ida's absence, the head servant. Though, in time, her sadness faded as she was groomed to be of a very obvious status with Master Butler. She went to check on Ida less and less, only going down to the quarters when she absolutely had to. On Butler, all eyes were on her, sending her chin a few notches higher and giving her the confidence of a First Lady, a role she had dreamed of since the first blood dripped between her legs.

The same feeling of loneliness Nella Jo felt in the confines of the small room behind the kitchen when she first moved there with baby Yuna, she felt then, walking alongside the river. The sun reflected the rust and crimson leaves across the waters, creating a companion of movement for her as she headed to Yuna's cabin. Halfway there, she noticed her daughter sitting on a large boulder a ways ahead. In front of her stood her father, as handsome as ever. The resemblance between the two reminded Nella Jo of the very small role she played in the link between them. The two of them were fine whether air slid through her lungs or not.

They were involved in an intense conversation, Yuna wailing her hands as she spoke, her father with his own in front of him, palms open. It was how he handled business. Once, he'd told her that a balled fist had something to hide, and a hidden hand in business hid even more. Nella Jo came closer, enough to strain herself to hear what they spoke about as she settled in behind the big live oak between them.

"But they are all the way in Philadelphia? Surely there must be Vines closer to here that can work with me. Philadelphia, its just...it's just so far away. And Grand. What about Grand Ida? There's no way I can be that far away from her. She needs me."

"I need you." Grayson kept his palms steady as his voice took a higher octave towards Yuna's whining. "I need you, Yuna, to get as far away from this place as you can so that you may get the best schooling my money can pay for. Now I have researched this Vines group. They only work with mulattos like yourself and very few Blacks. You cannot just walk into a school and pick up your education from where Mercy's best left off." He rested his hand on Yuna's shoulder. "Besides, Philadelphia is a good place. You'll see that the North has a much better life to offer than anything on either side of this river."

"Master Butler, I'll take another tutor, if you'll let me. I just can't bear the thought of my grandmother having no one. I have to be here, I just have to."

"She will have Nella Jo."

"In that case, she'll have no one plus the misery of my Mother." Yuna stood from the rock, losing her father's hand. "No thank you. I just cannot do that to her."

"Yuna!" Grayson was somewhere between a shout and grabbing her by the arm, ready to shake sense into the stubborn girl. Nella Jo could hear every word he said clearly after he called his daughter's name. "Do you realize any one of these people would give away half of their body and soul to have the opportunity I'm giving you?"

"Some of them already have. And my Grand is one of them." Yuna puffed up at her father, affording Nella Jo a slight smirk across her own face. Finally that girl had found a bit of her backbone, she only wished it had not been against her father. "I don't mean to sound disrespectful, or even ungrateful Master Butler, but I just can't leave Mercy. Not for school, not for anything. I just can't. Besides I got my own plans."

"You can and you will." Again, his voice carried.

Yuna turned to storm away like the spoiled child she was when she did not get things her way. It was always the wrong things she wanted. Why couldn't she use her position for more useful things than worrying about some old woman in a back cabin who would probably be dead long before the train Yuna would leave on reached the outskirts of Pennsylvania.

"I won't." Yuna turned to her father. "I am not your slave and you cannot just tell me to come and go as you please. I have a mind of my own, plans of my own, and you've provided me with the best education Mercy has to offer. I'm ready to make decisions for myself."

"In that stubbornness you carry, I've given you a right bit of my strong head, too, I see. So I expect you to resist. I'll give you that, girl, and a few days to think this over. But you will go and make a better life for yourself than the one waiting here for you."

"Is that what this is about Master Butler, you wanting me to live a life like the new Mrs. Butler. Lovely and proper? Marry well?"

"What do you mean? She's an educated woman. And one that's taking quite the liking to you, in spite of the circumstances."

Just then, Nella Jo felt a bitter taste in her mouth as she saw Mrs. Butler walking towards Yuna and Grayson. Of course she would show up. The woman was everywhere with her nose poked in everything going on around Butler. In the short time she'd been there, she knew more than the old Mrs. Butler had ever known about what went on. The old Mrs. Butler kept to her duties of being a wife and making sure her home ran smoothly. Anything outside of that, or anything she wished not to know about, she simply did not.

Grayson greeted her with a kiss to her cheek as she stopped the violent swinging of her hand fan long enough to receive his lips. Nella Jo hated to have seen it. He spoke in a more calm, lower tone now that she was in their presence and a part of their conversation. Before long, after straining her ears to hear, Nella Jo finally made out Mrs. Butler's words of encouragement to Yuna. She went on about how wonderful Philadelphia would be. Yuna barely spoke, the whole while looking back and forth between her father and her father's wife.

Nella Jo wondered if Yuna saw parents in the two of them. Where did she fit in amongst an already strained relationship between her and her daughter? She wanted badly to rush over and throw herself in the middle of what looked like the making of the family she was supposed to be a part of. Nella Jo had worked all the years since Yuna's birth to make what was forbidden real to keep herself happy and free of worry of anyone taking it away. And now, here she was, alone, spying on her own dream life from around the corner with loose bark pieces crumbling away at her hand.

chapter 11

SYLVIA DROPPED THE BOTTOM OF HER DRESS to the ground and brushed away the wrinkles from her apron. She watched Alivia jump from the raft in a childlike glee she never recalled having. "Well look at what the river brought over?" Yuna walked up just as Sylvia grabbed her basket from the ground.

"We heading over to Ida's." Sylvia said as Yuna stared at Alivia in a peculiar way. "This here is Alivia."

"I'm Alivia." Yuna and Sylvia both smiled at the child's introduction of herself with her arms wrapped behind her back, twisting her from side to side.

"And I'm Yuna. Nice to meet you." Yuna rubbed the girl's head. "Gran' seems to be in rare form this morning, Aunt Sylvia. She's more stiff today and less like herself. She hasn't been over here to the river in a few days. Maybe seeing you can get her out of that cabin." Yuna tapped at Alivia's nose. "And if that don't get her out, seeing this little button of sunshine will just have to do the trick."

"We'll see. Everybody knows you can't give an order to a chief."

Yuna was the only somebody on the Butler plantation Ida considered family. No one could blame her with the way her own daughter was busy being a First Lady with no time for her own mother. And Julius was no better.

Ida's cabin sat against the river, in the area deepest into the quarters, a shack smaller than the one Julius and Sylvia shared. The one stair, with a hole in it between the earth and a washboard porch where rain and time had rotted it away, seemed to be getting bigger. Everyone knew to step over it. Sylvia used the wooden post that held the porch upright to pull herself up over it. Her body was not as fragile as Ida's but it was definitely not in new and sturdy condition.

"Come on in, Sylvia." Ida sat in the same chair as always, today, facing the door. Her eyes were closed and her head rested against the back of the chair. She didn't need to see a person to know who they were. Ida had been around long enough to know to use all her senses when it came to knowing someone and having them in your presence.

"You resting?"

"I'm old." She laughed a small bit. "I'm always resting. Sound better than telling folk you waiting to die."

"Oh Ms. Ida." Sylvia laughed. Her sense of humor kept her sane all these years. That, a two by four, and a feisty attitude. "This here..."

"You got a child with you? Who young'n is that?" With her eyes still closed, she adjusted herself in her chair. "I know you and my boy ain't still cross that river makin' babies."

"Oh no ma'am." Sylvia shivered at the thought of her own babies.

"Probably ain't doing nothing over there to make no babies." This time Ida laughed loud, a lot, and slapped at her knee. Finally she opened her eyes, slowly. Age had stolen the color from them as the milky balls focused on Sylvia and Alivia standing in the doorway.

"Well come on in. Let me get a good look 'atcha." She motioned to the girl. Alivia moved forward in a slow pace so the old woman could see her better. "Who child this? She sure got the smell of me on her." Sylvia was embarrassed to tell Ida she knew nothing other than she was responsible for taking care of Alivia by Julius orders.

"She got honey on her."

"No ma'am. I only had the molasses on my biscuit." Alivia corrected Ida.

"That's not what she means, babygirl."

"You got that right. Sure ain't what I mean. I mean in your blood. But you don't look like you old enough to know nothing 'bout that. How old you anyway?"

"I'm four and five." Alivia looked at Sylvia and smiled.

"Well you a good looking girl, don't let none of these evils out here spoil you over." Ida grunted, sitting back in her chair. " You hear what I tell you?"

Taking a step back, Alivia said, "Yes ma'am." She sat on the floor, crossed her legs and started playing with the end of her braid.

"What bring you cross here?" Ida asked Sylvia, who was taking a seat on the bench near the wall. "And I see you got yourself a limp?"

"Yes." Sylvia said under her breath, hating to acknowledge it.

"Well you ain't old enough for your bones to be turning on you yet, so I take it my boy give it to you?" Sylvia formed her mouth to say yes, but before the word made it out, Julius' mother interrupted. "Don't answer that. I already know. Besides, where ever you get it, ain't good, so don't really matter no how."

Sylvia sighed. "Came over to talk with you about herbs."

"Herbs?" Ida frowned her nose up. "What you need with me and herbs? You know more 'bout the ground and what it give us than most people on this here plantation and the next. What ailing you?"

Sylvia thought for a moment, then said the words in her mind. If there was anywhere in the world she could speak free it was with Ida. She had given Sylvia advice on many things, including how to deal with Julius. All failed, but she admired her and valued her opinion nonetheless. Sylvia loved Ida for even believing there was any one way to deal with a man.

"A white woman ailing me."

"White woman?" She grunted again, eyes closed. "Your white lady over there giving you hell?"

"Something like that." Sylvia shifted on the bench to give herself a bit more comfort against the hard seat. "You know anything about the Kifo, Ms. Ida?"

"Lawd, how much trouble your white woman giving you?!" She sat straight up in her chair and opened her eyes, trying to focus. "Nuff to get you thinking you wanna kill her off?"

"No." She tried not to raise Ida's suspicion any more than she already had. "Just wondering about it."

"You over there in that white lady books again? That where you hear about the Kifo? Cause that ain't no regular sprinkle on your stew kinda herb you asking me 'bout, girl."

"I know what it is. I just..." Sylvia remained calm and tried not to react to Ida's reaction.

"Then you know it the kind that mean you mad as hell, fed up, and tired and ready to make a big old change in somebody life. That's the start of what I know about it. Now how much more you trying to find out?" She eased back into the chair and crossed her hands over her stomach.

"Where you find something like that?"

Again, she popped up from the chair, this time gripping the sides and sitting forward as if she was ready to push off into a full launch. "Look here child, you go on outside and find something to do." She directed Alivia. "And watch yourself on that there hole in the step. Get your foot caught in there and pull it clean off."

Alivia left the cabin without a fuss, happy to go outside on her own.

"Now what're you up to, Sylvia. And don't go giving me the ass end of your story."

Sylvia told her everything. Ida laughed long and hard when Sylvia finished telling her about Mistress' plan. "You mean to tell me that white woman done give up on trying to fight her husband and now she want you to kill him. Then what? They gone string you up and she gone go on about her life." Ida grunted and settled back into her chair. "Well, I tell you this. This crazy life here come with it share of open doors."

"What does that mean?"

"Sylvia. You got nearly just as much wise gray on your head as I got on mine and you just barely at half my age." She sucked at her teeth. "I ain't got to tell you nothing more than what I just said. You got sense enough to know what to do with it."

She was right. Sylvia knew exactly what Ida meant. She just wanted someone to tell her flat out what to do. She wanted to hear Ida say 'do it Sylvia' or 'don't mess with that Sylvia', but the decision was hers. At the same time, she knew this open door she was standing in front of could be her opportunity. Not her opportunity to be free of Julius, but somehow she could talk with Mistress and make this work out for her advantage. Times were changing, but in ways that were teetering between worse and more worse for Blacks. The freedom they prayed all of their lives for was giving them more pain than slavery had. What they needed now was mercy. And that was exactly what she intended to ask Mistress to give her. If she was going to put her neck on the line in such a way for her, Mistress was going to, for once, do a little bit more for her.

Sylvia got up from the bench and leaned in on her walking stick. It felt smoother in her hand than it had before. Standing beside Ida, she rubbed the head of the woman who had been like a mother to her. The thinning hair laid down, untroubled, against her head. With her eyes still closed, Ida smiled at Sylvia's presence. She leaned over and kissed her on the side of her pleated cheek. "Thank you."

"What you thanking me for? I ain't give you what you came here for."

"You're right, Ms Ida. You gave me what I needed though." Sylvia said. "I can work the rest out for myself."

⋯◦◦◦⋯

The cabins were quiet when Sylvia and Alivia arrived back on the Purvis side of the river. Every bone in Sylvia's body ached, but the girl was full of energy and words. It had been a few weeks since the night Alivia arrived with watery eyes and a runny nose in the cookhouse, but she was still a mystery. Sylvia had yet to figure out where Alivia had come from? Even more, how long would she stay?

"Livy?"

"Ma'am?" She twirled around a few steps ahead of Sylvia.

"Who your momma?"

"Opal. And Fedil my Papa. He bring me here to your place. But momma say it's just for a little while."

"You know where they live? Where you call home?"

"Waters. We live on the Waters plan-a-ta-tion."

"Plantation."

"Yes, plantation." Alivia said the word the second time with a confidence of knowing it as she twirled in a circle.

Sylvia vowed silently to herself, if nothing else, for however long Alivia was hers, she would protect her and do her best to keep the girl's spirit whole. She pulled her from her twirl and sucked her up in her arms while the little girl giggled up to the sky.

At that very moment as they walked the path towards the cabins, she thought of The Collector. It'd been a long while since she had seen the wagon come around, not since the Yankees. Sylvia was thankful money could no longer be made from selling Negros so a child was free to grow in the bosom of her mother.

"What if the day came when Opal and Fedil returned for their daughter and she would have to give her back?", she thought... "What if?" As young as Sylvia was, she was too old for another broken heart. This time it just might not mend.

At home, Julius had not arrived yet. With the spare time, Sylvia and Alivia took a seat on the small porch. Alivia sat one step below Sylvia and played with a leaf she had picked up along the way home. She folded it forward and backwards, unfolding it to start all over again. Taking a moment to glance away from her, Sylvia spotted Julius coming up the path. She stood up, using the walking stick that was becoming a permanent part of her life more than she wanted it to be, and went inside to begin preparations for supper.

By the time Julius came in, Sylvia was nearly done chopping the few vegetables she had left from the garden. "Dinner be ready in a short while," she said, pulling a few pieces of okra from her pocket she took from the cookhouse and chopping them into the medley.

Julius flopped down into the chair without a word. She waited for his response, she waited to figure out what kind of mood he was in. Some days, talking too much landed her a backhand slap. Other days, he had so much to say, but just needed a little quiet time to get his head together to say it.

So she chopped and stirred and made the clinking dishes their conversation.

"This place killing me," he finally said. Another moment or two passed. "Mercy gone be the death of me."

The thought of his body in a pine box sent a chill up Sylvia's spine mixed in with relief and sorrow. She busied herself with stirring at the vegetables in the small pot, keeping her eyes away from him. "We been here all this while and we still alive."

She waited for more, already knowing what he meant. He was tired. He was frustrated. Not with Mercy so much as with being Black. He had spent his entire life as a slave. So many times as a young boy, he tried to run away from plantations, the life he was dealt as a slave, only to be caught, returned, and forced deeper into the life he'd tried to leave. Then the news of freedom came, and Julius grasped onto hope. A few years later, life was still the same. They were still on a plantation. They still worked from sun up to sun down. And they still had nothing to show for it. There was no way out. Mercy was it.

The few who had made it to Hartha Gables, were favored or lucky. Some had had White folks who had looked out for them and sent word ahead against any travel hardship until safe arrival. And then still, there were the White folks who had profited off of their former slaves by bribing patrollers to leave them be, with the promise that once the former slaves settled north, they'd work and pay off the debt of their owners' kind words for their safety - only for some Blacks to pay even more than they could ever work off just to get free from their masters. Mistress herself had said she would help Sylvia. She wondered if any of them had been asked to take a life in order to gain their freedom. Another chill went through her body.

All this, Julius would never say. All this, Sylvia would never say.

Julius walked up behind her at the stove. She dared not turn around, but tried to feel what his spirit was up to. And though his tone was calm, she could feel the sting of venom at her neck.

"Been here all my life, but ain't gone die here. And sure ain't gone die with you on my back holding me down."

Sylvia heard him go back to sit at the table. The okra slimmed in the mix of herbs and other vegetables. They were done, nearing over cooked, but she just could not move herself.

When she plated the vegetables in front of him, he stared forward. She took another small plate to the porch, where Alivia was still playing with the leaves. She was happy and content and Sylvia wanted her to stay that way. "You eat your supper out here tonight, okay? Do as I tell you."

Inside, Julius was standing, facing the door, facing her. Sylvia's heart pounded in a rhythm she knew all too well. She braced herself against the door.

He came closer, hand drawn back.

She closed her eyes.

She landed on the floor crossing the doorway.

The room blurred.

His figure grew in the spinning.

Then the yanking of her hair.

The dragging of her lifeless body across the floor to the potato sack wall dividing the bedroom from the rest of the house, from the rest of the world.

Sylvia could hear and worse, feel the roots of her hair tearing from her scalp.

The door opened.

Her own drowning voice ordered, "Go. Go back outside. Go, Livy."

The bed pallet under her back.

The pounding on her head, face, neck.

The silence inside of herself as she repeated the scripture in what was left of her mind.

"Yea, though I walk through the valley of the shadow of death, I will fear no evil: for thou art with me; thy rod and thy staff, they comfort me."

The stillness of her body.

The walking stick in her view but out of her reach.

Her eyes rested in the corner, in the depth of it, as he pounded her until she slid into blackness with thoughts of the little girl outside, alone and without her.

chapter 12

FROM HER BEDROOM, Nella Jo heard Master Butler walk into the kitchen, then out of it. She hurried to wrap her robe around her naked body in the moonlight's view of her open window to see if there was a need she could fulfill, a moment to spend in his presence. Rushing through the kitchen, she burst through the door that connected it to the parlor to find him in his usual chair.

"Gray..Master Butler, is there anything you need? I heard you stir in the kitchen." The words eased past her heart and between longing breaths. Her fingers, clutched the ball of closure she held together in front of her robe, another gift from him in a time which felt long ago.

He glared at her, a slight smirk, no words. The silence between them, invaded only by her own heavy, yet controlled breathing, lingered. His shaking foot, crossed atop his knee, told her he was relaxed. His left hand rested on the crossed leg, a gold band on his ring finger. She looked past it. She looked past the man he had been to her since his return, a Master, an employer. With a stolen look here and there, three nights of absent passion beneath her bedsheets, it had been just enough to hold onto, and to let go of. Nella Jo broke the silence with the clearing of her throat.

"Master Butler." She regained the composure his gaze worked to steal away. "I take it there is nothing you need, so I'll just return to my room." She turned and headed for the kitchen door only to be reeled back in the baritone of his voice.

"Nella Jo."

With an inhale, a palm against the door, she turned back to him. "Yes, sir."

"No need for formalities. She's asleep."

"What I am giving is not formality, sir." She stressed the title of his position. "It's merely an acknowledgement of how things are...now." Again, she clutched at her robe, holding in her bare body and the rapid beating heart he created in simply being present.

"I am still Grayson Butler."

"That I know."

"Father of our child."

"As well you are. Though, let us not forget your new self, husband to the sleeping Mrs. Butler just upstairs."

The smirk he had held since she entered the room turned to a full smile. He stood and moved closer to her from the other side of the room. All at once, she wanted to run away and stay. Her heart continued its gallop against her bosom. When he was closer, sharing breath with her, she did not know who she was to be in the moment, his lover, mother of his only child, or his wife's maidservant in charge of the house and kitchen staff.

Or, the forgotten one.

He placed his hand beneath her chin, the same hand bearing the band given to him by his wife. Nella Jo turned away, refusing to be pulled into a night of lovemaking without love or her.

"So you resist me now."

"As you have me since your return?"

"Nella Jo."

"Grayson."

He took a step back and examined the new woman before him. He wanted to crawl into her robe and forget the world. She was still beautiful to him. Her skin smooth as silk, glistened.

"You know why I did that, why I married her?"

"Her skin is pale like yours and mine is not."

"She loves me, as well."

"She loves your money, Grayson. The woman has done nothing more than shop and complain since she arrived."

"Nella Jo."

She did not respond but watched him and he looked at her. There within the silence, without moving and touching they crashed into each other, wrapped themselves tight until they were lost in sheer affection and longing.

"Nella Jo." This time, in a softer, gentle tone and a step closer, again. "Times have not changed out there no matter what we feel for each other. They never will. I had to marry...I'm no young man."

"You were mine."

He wished he could fight the world for her.

"Here. Inside this house. On this plantation. But out there, in the world, in reality, in front of townspeople and everyone else, I am a man getting older with no bride. I could only tell the story of mourning my past wife for so many years."

"Nineteen."

"Yes, nineteen years she has been gone."

"Nineteen years I have been your lover, First Lady, and mother to your only child. And this is how you love me, now? In this way? As a servant? As a bedmate in the late hour when your picture wife does nothing for your heart?" She released her grip on her robe, exposing whatever the opening permitted. In that moment what she cared about most was letting him know what she had been holding in her head since his return. "I'm a servant ...no, no. Grayson, I am your slave, the young girl in the cabin when you would call for me, make love to me, and send me on my way. That is all I am to you now. Admit it!"

"I will not."

"You will! You will admit that is all you see in me now. Admit it!"

"Nella Jo you will lower your voice this instant!" Then, he was her master, scolding and commanding her. Silencing her. Tears fell from her eyes in the dark room. Again, he took a step back, his eyes still on her in the poorly lit room. "You are more than that."

"Then why are you taking everything away from me?" Any other woman would be in a full sob, pleading for the love of her heart. Nella Jo simply let the tears fall from her eyes, still managing to keep her voice even, her head held up to him.

"What do you mean by that? What have I taken from you? No one has taken anything from you. Are you not still living in your room here in this house? Do you not still have the freedom to come and go as you please? Are you not..."

"Where would I go? Where am I to go? I have nothing but this life you groomed me for and a rebellious daughter you are now trying to send away." She wiped her eyes with the back of her hand and returned to clutching her robe shut. Seeing the look in Grayson's eyes, she knew he wondered how she knew about Philadelphia. "Yes, I know of you trying to send her away from here."

"I thought you wanted the best for our daughter."

"I do."

"Then what. Is it not best to send her to the Vines? Even the best of Mercy's tutors have taken her as far as they are capable of with her studies. She cannot go off to an ivy league school as if her skin was solely the color of mine. The Vines are the next best thing. Why do you not agree?"

"Because she is all I have left." He looked at her, finally dropping her face into her hands. There were no words he could offer her. It was true. They both wanted what was best for Yuna, but it had never crossed his mind Nella Jo would react this way. She lifted her soggy face to him. "I do want what is best for her, but have mercy on me that I want to have something to hold onto, even if she does challenge the very air I breathe." She wiped at her eyes, grasped her robe again. "I must go."

"Nella Jo." He called after her, the kitchen door swinging, and then the sound of her bedroom door closing shut.

The next morning, Nella Jo folded the blanket and placed it neatly at the foot of the bed. Outside the open window in Mrs. Butler's room she could hear the shrieking laugh of the pale woman's voice from the front porch below. The laugh was too loud, too tortuous on the ears.

"And then the foolish woman carried on for hours about nothing." Mrs. Butler broke out into a laugh along with the two women, wives of townsmen, following suit.

Nella Jo shook her head and closed the window. "Yes she did," she mumbled under her breath before leaving the room and heading downstairs. In the kitchen, Yuna sat at the table reading a book.

"Afternoon darling."

"Mother."

Yuna's bitter word rose from pages of what looked like a child's picture book. She scribbled words on a paper beside her, then back to the book.

Nella Jo watched suspicious, curious. When she could take it no longer, she had to ask. "What are you doing?"

"Reading."

"Well there don't seem to be many words on the book. In fact, is that not a book for a small child."

"If you must know," Yuna closed the book and laid her pencil on the table, irritated. "I'm planning."

Nella Jo said nothing and Yuna offered nothing more. They stared at each other like cats waiting to pounce. Finally, Nella Jo broke. "Oh for Heaven's sake, why are you playing such a guessing game with me. Do you want to tell me or not?"

"No, I don't want to tell you, but I know that if I don't, you'll just keep snooping and asking until I do. So here," she slid the paper she was writing on over to her mother. "That is what I am going to teach."

"Teach?" Nella Jo glanced at the page only long enough to see the list of letters and words across the page. "What do you mean teach? And to who are you planning to teach?"

"Whom?"

"What?"

"It's to whom are you going to teach." Yuna gave a slight smirk and opened the book again, reaching for her paper and scribbling once again.

"Well, I did not have the fortune of having a fine father to bring in a tutor to teach me the who and whom of my question, which you still did not answer." She waited.

"Have not answered." Yuna wrote another set of words on her paper.

"Yuna." Nella Jo allowed Yuna's corrections to cross her. She took a breath. "To whom will you be teaching this list of words."

"People like you."

"Excuse me."

"People like you." She closed the book again, this time turning to her mother. "It's just like you said, everyone has not had the fortune of private tutoring as I have. So I want to share what I've learned with others. Children, elders, anyone. Even you, if you want."

"Me? Oh no, I do believe I am beyond the age of learning new tricks. Besides, I have a house to run and a white lady to…"

"Mother."

Nella Jo held her tongue. "So, this teaching you're planning to do in Philadelphia…"

"In Philadelphia?"

"Yes. That is where you will be heading …am I right?"

"I won't even bother with asking how you know about Philadelphia, but to answer your question, no. I plan to do my teaching right here. In Mercy." Yuna's innocence covered her face and lifted the high cheekbones she had inherited from Nella Jo, raising the freckles her father had given her. She was oblivious to the reality of the times. They may have been free but reading and learning and all those other things were still frowned upon by the people of Mercy.

chapter 13

SYLVIA DIDN'T CARE HER KNEES HURT. It did not even bother her to find she had cut two of her fingers on bladed thorns. Collecting the ingredients for Kifo tea mattered more.

Stuffing the herbs in an inside pocket of her apron, though, made her eyes grow as heavy with water as the hovering clouds. There was no time for crying, no time for messing up the recipe. Making Kifo tea required complete attention. Every detail of the process had to be done right, everything must be measured right, and given at the right time for intake. She took a deep breathe and blinked hard sending the tears away.

It was from the mouth of her own mother she first heard the word 'Kifo' and it wasn't until later she learned what the Kifo truly was.

Raindrops soaked through her headscarf to her scalp as she got up from the riverbank, patted both her pockets to make sure nothing could fall out, and headed back to the cabin. Today she was glad Ida was feeling better than she had been. The fever they both thought was going to take her away from them had finally broke and she was getting back to her old self. She had asked for Alivia to help raise her spirits back to where they belong. The two had begun to take a liking to each other, spending afternoons together more and more often. Sylvia was glad the child was not by her side, those eyes and curious mind would sense her anxiety. There was just enough light left in the sky for Sylvia to make it home before Julius arrived from town. This Sunday evening belonged only to what she had to do.

"Don't you set a sprig of nothing in that pot 'fore the water roarin' up at you," she could hear her mother's voice.

Sylvia added a few more pieces of coal to the flame and waited, listening to the dying storm outside the cabin. The little piece of Bible trembled in her hands as she read by the fire's light. If she was going to hell for what she was doing, helping to do, she wanted to make sure the good Lord knew that she still believed in his Word til the end of her days.

He is all knowing and must understand it had to be done, she thought. She figured if she did not help Mistress and get them out of Mercy, Julius would kill her one day soon. She knew she would not be able to withstand another spit of tobacco juice in her face, another kick in her chest, and most of all bear the look of Alivia's eyes before each black-out. As much as she must have hurt in her body, her soul ached at the wonder of what Julius, drunk and violent, would do to the little girl if she tried to rescue her.

Sylvia stoked the fire, looked inside the big black pot at the tiny bubbles, black themselves and bursting with the sharp and earthy stench. It began to boil, so Sylvia picked up the Bible again.

Beloved, never avenge yourselves, but leave it to the wrath of God, for it is written, "Vengeance is mine, I will repay, says the Lord."

But this book of Romans, twelfth chapter, nineteenth verse, did not speak of her lack of time. She felt there was no more time to wait on the Lord. There was Mistress and her urgent pleas and nagging, pestering her to find out if she planned to do it. The largest reason was the last beating Julius gave her, in front of Alivia, who watched her bend to each blow and left on the floor with no regard. Her whole life, she waited on the Lord to protect her and He did sure in sparing her life through every moment of pain given to her by Julius, Master Purvis, and anybody else who had ever hurt her. Maybe He saved her life so she could be there to make sure no harm came to the child. Thoughts whirled around her head, fast and furious. With her whole heart, she accepted those reasons, being what they were. Good enough!

"Thorns gotta be soft," her mother's voice again. "Gotta take the prickly out of 'em before you can mash out the insides. Use the back of a fork so you don't waste none. When you done with that, measure out a palmful and you wrap it in a piece of fig leaf and sit it out in the south corner, the way you lay your head in the moonlight. It gotta 'bsorb all that it need to do the deed from the moon, you hear? Best if full moon, but nothing less than a wanin' moon. The fuller the better."

Outside, in the soaked ground at the south corner of the cabin, Sylvia tucked the fig leaf beneath a loose oak board. It fit in with the mess blown around in the rain and winds. The night was more calm and quiet than any other night in the quarters with everyone inside after the rain, and resting for the next morning. She sat on the porch and pulled her dress down between open legs. In her pocket, she touched at the sprigs from the only bush of its kind in Mercy, just to make sure they were still there. They could not touch the thorn mesh before it was ready otherwise the Kifo would be no more harmful than a warm cup of jasmine or blackberry tea. In her other pocket, where the thorns had been, she'd stuffed the Bible pages, but under the moon's stare, she was too nervous to pull them out of it.

Morning woke Sylvia up with Julius' arm wrapped around her waist and his heavy breathing on the back of her neck. The number of times she was awakened in his embrace would be less than the number of children she birthed. More surprising was the missing stench of corn liquor.

When she was up ready to head to the cookhouse, she noticed the brown paper bag he always carried sitting on the table. In disbelief, she lifted the forbidden bag making little noise. It felt heavy, full.

All of her thoughts and wondering walked her to the cookhouse, her hand gripped around the fig pouch. They swirled all over as she began to go about her work.

"Silva!"

She jumped at Mistress' voice.

"Ma'am? You like to scare me half to death and make me spill this here water all over the place." Sylvia sat the pail next to the well house door and stretched her back. "And why in the devil you out here in your night britches this time of morning? You sick?"

Mistress cupped her hand to the side of her mouth in a whisper so much so Sylvia strained to hear. "A lot of time has passed, Silva, and I haven't heard anything from you other than a new wince you make when you are bent down for the chamber pots. How much longer are you going to need to think? I never known a Negro to do this much thinking." She dropped her whispering hand.

"You been studying me, Mistress?"

"I'm observant."

"Besides, Silva, you and I, we look out for each other."

Sylvia kept her thoughts to herself about the two of them looking out for each other. There had been times Mistress had covered for her to Master Purvis and the overseer when she was ailing bad in the back of the cookhouse in pain, nursing wounds. And there had been times Mistress had lied to Master Purvis and others that inquired of her whereabout, why she had not come down for breakfast or afternoon tea when Sylvia knew Mistress felt a spell coming on or had a bruise makeup powder could not cover. If Mistress considered times as those looking out for each other, then they did. It was what they had.

"Yes, we do, ma'am."

"So tell me, how much longer is it going to take for you to make up that mind of yours to agree that I know what's best for us?" She tugged on the top of her night dress and looked back towards the main house. "You know, I don't know about you, but I don't know how much more of this I can take. Just last night, Early got into an awful upset when I mentioned visiting Sister this upcoming weekend. If it weren't for the mercy of God, I do believe the chamber pot he tossed at me would've cracked my skull right open."

"Mistress, we will talk." Sylvia followed her gaze towards the main house. "But not here, and not right now."

Just then, Nan came waddling out of the cookhouse.

"Syl, you coming with that water or baptizing yourself--" She stopped short.

"Oh, I'm sorry Mistress! I didn't..."

Then she gave the most awful version of a curtsy a big body could give. Sylvia cupped her hand to her mouth to stop the laughter tickling her throat.

"Go back in, Nan," said Mistress. "I'm talking to Silva."

"Yes ma'am." Another awful curtsy.

Once Nan was gone, Mistress turned back to Sylvia.

"Tonight, you stay late and I will walk with you."

"You?" Sylvia caught her voice rising and fixed her tone. "Uh, you, Mistress, walk with me where?"

"To the path by the river."

"At night, ma'am? Hardly sounds like a good idea."

"Well we can't discuss anything here."

Sylvia sighed. "Here's what we'll do. I will meet you here, behind the cookhouse, on that stoop over there. But, Mistress, you gone to have to be real quiet and pay good attention to what I tell you."

"But of course." Her face lit up and a pink glow covered her face.

Alivia sat on the porch while Sylvia worked her garden, pulling weeds and saving what was left of the herbs in the dry weather. Not until she was nearly done with her work did she notice the girl balled in a corner, waving her hand at a leaf. The way she hit at it seemed peculiar to Sylvia. Curious, she stopped pulling at the ground, and listened.

"You make me do this to you. If you would just do as I tell you, we wouldn't…"

"Livy!"

Alivia stopped slapping at the leaf. Defenseless, it sagged back and forth against her small hand.

"What're you doing?"

The girl dropped the leaf to the wooden porch and looked away but turned her eyes to their corners in Sylvia's direction. Sylvia got up from the ground and sat beside her. By the time she made her way into a comfortable sitting position, Alivia had slid a few inches aside.

"What's the matter?"

Still, Alivia did not respond. When she reached for the girl's hand, not only did she flinch, but she pulled away and held her head as if she were about to be struck.

In an instant faster than light, Sylvia grew strong. The scars on her own body would scab and heal in time and maybe fade into the back of her mind. It was the life she had come to know, but for Alivia this was all new, frightening and soon it would change her eyes to accept it. Sylvia let her head rest against the wall separating the outside from the inside of the small cabin, searching her thoughts for words of comfort to say. Nothing came to her.

She did not dare to reach for Alivia again, not wanting to scare her any more than she was already. The only thing to make the child feel safe again would be to protect her from what she feared, to show her a different way to live. Sure enough, Julius was down at Chewy's getting liquored up and ready for a night to break her the way he was broken. It was Friday. The work week for him was at an end and he wanted to sulk and celebrate all at once in a jar of whatever Chewy served him. Sylvia thought of the taste of the liquor he'd made her drink and shivered in the evening heat.

Nan had offered to finish things at the cookhouse with Dollet so Sylvia could end her day early and get home in time enough to let the child play in the daylight a while. Alivia was far from playing. She was already cinched up in places by fear and she did not know what to do with it but let it travel in her to fight a leaf.

When Julius arrived, as suspected, he was very drunk. He staggered onto the porch past Alivia, still in the same spot, refusing to move inside. Sylvia went in to put on some food for the girl, but she did not want to eat. Sylvia even offered to let her stir the pot, which Alivia had come to enjoy while working with Dollet. The offer brought about no thrill for the girl as she continued her play with a fallen branch. She stripped the limbs of its leaves with fierce movements, too violent for a child. It saddened Sylvia even more.

"Sylvia!" Julius shouted slamming the door behind himself. "Get here!" Standing right in the same room as he was, she felt the muscles of her neck tense. The way he yelled told her his state of mind. He was upset about something and she would pay the price for it.

"You was 'posed to be down at Chewy's wit' me da'night."

"Julius, I don't go down there. You know that. That's yo' place to go an' unwind." She placed a gentle hand on his shoulder and smiled the words out of her mouth, hoping he would succumb to her sweetness. "How was ya night?"

He pushed her hand away from him, staggering a few steps then catching his balance. She was glad Alivia had chosen to stay outside. "Meeting tonight and...and...and..."

She waited for his words to stop fighting with his teeth and tongue, all the while keeping her eye on the door he just entered. Sylvia prayed for God to keep the girl outside, in the quiet evening. She prayed for Julius to fall asleep before the moment grew into terror, large and ugly.

"...and meeting was tonight and ev'ybody goin' on out of here 'cept us. Even that Samson say he thinkin' bout takin' up and leavin' with' his ...his…"

"His wife?" Sylvia said the words trying to help Julius along.

"Don't you mock me, woman!"

"Oh no, no Julius. I was just tryin'a help." She raised a surrendering hand to him. He looked at her hand as if it pushed some kind of spell on him. His eyes crossed then uncrossed. He staggered backwards then forward into another stagger. When he managed to grip the table beside him to steady his sway, he was even more furious. "You got us stuck in this here hell! You!" He was yelling again, louder. She was sure Alivia was as scared outside as Sylvia was in front of her angry husband.

She looked at the door again, making sure it did not open even a little. Distracted, she missed Julius picking up the half empty pot from the table and she missed him slinging it at her head. When the blow hit her, she fell to the floor. Dizzy, she held the side of her head and tried to keep quiet, to swallow the pain.

Julius wobbled and tried to lean forward, swinging his fist toward Sylvia, but missed. Before he could gain his composure, she drug her body behind him, knowing it would take him a while to collect himself and turn. By the time he did, she had made her way to her knees and crawled out of his reach. He bent forward to grab at her foot, but just as he did, he lost his balance and fell. With a hard thump, he yelled every curse word at her he could. She got up and ran for the door. Outside, she reached for a crying Alivia. When she realized the hand she extended to the child was stained with blood from her head, she wiped at her apron. Alivia stayed huddled with her knees drawn to her face. Sylvia could hear Julius stirring inside the house. There was no time to spare. She reached down and grabbed Alivia up in to her arms, slinging the child's legs around both sides of her hip and did the best she could to run without the help of her walking stick. The ground moved a bit in her disoriented mind. Alivia kept quiet as the tears ran down her face.

"Ma Syl gotta put you down babygirl," she said when they were far enough from the house to know Julius was not chasing behind them. He had more than likely passed out before stepping off of the porch. She dug her palms into her lower thigh and caught her breath. Alivia pointed to her head, blood still flowing from the gash. In all the haste, Sylvia had not even taken the time to wipe it away. She undid the tie on her apron and balled the material into a rag, pressing it against her head. Reaching for Alivia's hand, they went on toward the cookhouse.

The sound of Creek's gallop awoke Sylvia with a blade of grass sealed to her face, along with matted strings of hair, sweat, and blood. Her dress stuck to her body as she looked around, frantic and searching for something or someone to tell her what had happened to her. And where was Alivia? Where was everyone? She picked up her aching body from the ground, then realized she was behind the main house, on the path between it and the cookhouse. The gravel poked through her worn dress and pockmarked her thighs and forearms.

Somehow, she made her way to the cookhouse, moonlight beaming through the cross-boards. Inside, she dipped her bloody headscarf into a pail of water she was sure Dollet had forgot to empty. She reminded the girl more times than she could remember to toss out the pail at the end of the night. There was a knot on the side of her cheek and it felt to be the size of a young lime. She could not let Alivia find her in such a mess, though the lump was one she would not be able to cover. She wiped her face and dabbed at the tender, raised area.

"Surely, it had been Julius," she thought.

For the first time, though, she could not remember what happened. How in the name of Heaven and earth did she end up faced-down on the ground? And where was everyone?

As she wrung the scarf in the water, again, Sylvia heard a slight sniffle.

"Alivia?"

There she was, under the table, knees drawn tight against her chest the way they had been on the porch earlier. Her arms were locked around her as though she were hiding from a monster.

"Oh God! Come here, child."

She tugged easy at her arm. Alivia moved out and latched onto Sylvia's leg for dear mercy. "What's the matter? Tell me what happen? Why you cryin'?"

"Him." She muttered between sniffles and watery eyes.

"Was it Julius, babygirl? A stranger? An old White mean master? Who?" Sylvia began to pray inside so nothing would happen to Alivia and hoped she would not remember it. There were many memories, painful and horrid, she had shoved into the back of her own mind, never to will to the surface. But this, this could not be one of them.

Sylvia and Alivia both leaped into the corner of the room when Master Purvis burst through the cookhouse door, almost breaking it off the hinges. Sylvia tucked the child behind her.

"You, nappyheaded gal! You think you smart. You and that Negro-loving wife of mine plotting to kill me and take my money. I'll kill you both before I let either one of you poor excuses for women make a threat of any kind on my life!"

His soup-bowl face was red and peppered with sweat. The glasses he wore were absent and Sylvia saw his frigid eyeballs.

"Tell me, girl! Tell me what you put in that tea!"

"Master Purvis, sir, I...I..."

"If a lie comes out of your mouth, I'll beat the truth out of you one way or another. So think long and hard before you--"

"Sir, I don't know!" She was too concerned for Alivia to watch her tone or swear on God's name. "I don't know what in Lord's name you talking 'bout."

Master Purvis came closer, pressing Sylvia and Alivia both deeper into the corner.

"Gal, you gone tell me you don't know anything about the tea Vivian been trying to give me? Are you gonna tell me that your Mistress, who done give you the best life I let her give you, is a liar?"

His voice made Sylvia's head throb even more. He moved closer to her and when he was right in her face, enough for her to smell his sour breath and feel the spit from his words on her mouth, Sylvia pressed further into the corner. She kept her hand on Alivia. It was the only assurance she could provide the child of how she would be a shield for her small, trembling body.

He struck Sylvia.

Something inside kept her standing and her hand still on Alivia. When she opened her eyes to meet his, Master Purvis struck her again, harder.

"You're one uppity nigger that think I won't turn my back to the law and put you back in your place."

Sylvia's eyes met his. This only made him ball his hand into a fist this time and strike her to the floor. Alivia screamed and before either of them knew it, the girl lunged at Master Purvis.

With the back of his hand, he knocked her small body backwards and she slid across the floor. Her little body did not move from where it landed. Sylvia pushed pass Master Purvis on her hands and knees. Before she could fully raise Alivia into her arms, Master Purvis grabbed her by the throat and slung her back against the floor. There was an awakened place in her and she managed to get to her knees with her hand pressed into the table and lifted herself back to her feet. Blood poured from the side of her head, from her nose, and down her arm. When she rose to her feet, it was only long enough for her to feel his hand strike her back to the floor. Her head hit the corner of the table and everything began to go black. She heard his voice. Then another voice. She could not decipher what was real and what was not. In delirium, she pleaded with God to take care of Alivia just as she drifted away to a place all too familiar.

Sylvia awoke to tiny embroidered flowers on her chest.

"Who buries their dead with embroidered flowers?" was her first thought. Then she remembered the same flowers on Mistress' dress and when she spoke to the seamstress in town to purchase the material years ago. Sylvia tried to open both her eyes to see if she was in a strange heaven, wearing Mistress' dress, but she could only open one eye. The other was too bruised. The something soft under her head felt like the pillows she had fluffed for Mistress's bed. She tried to look around to see where she was.

Alivia. Sylvia remembered Master Purvis hitting her and in a panic tried to sit up. A familiar voice told her not to, "Don't try to move around. Only make things worse."

"Where..." It wasn't until Sylvia spoke she realized her lip was bulging like a cow udder. "Where 'Livy?"

"Stop trying to talk." That voice, it was Yuna. "Livy is fine. She's asleep. You and her both need rest. Just lay there and relax, Aunt Sylvia."

She finally saw Yuna walk past the one place she could see, the armoire in Mistress' bedroom.

What was she doing in Mistress' bedroom? And laying down? Mistress and Master Purvis both would kill her dead! Sylvia tried to get up but every aching and throbbing part of her body refused.

"Aunt Sylvia, please just lay down." Yuna placed the covers across her.

"Child," Sylvia said, "you tryin' to get us both..." Her lips could do no more. Her thoughts completed what her mouth could not.

Yuna's hand rested on her aunt's shoulder, trying to settle her.

"This ain't alright, layin' up in this house, Yuna. I got to get up from here. You know what gone happen if Mistress catch me here."

"Yes, I do. She's going to tell you to lay back and rest yourself awhile." Mistress walked into Sylvia's view. "And stop trying to talk so much. That lip of yours is something awful and need more of that salve on it."

"Mistress? You gone crazy, too?" Sylvia desperately wanted a drink of water.

"Hardly." She laughed in such a relaxed way.

"Water, please." Sylvia finally gave in to closing her one eye and laid back. "Mistress," she sighed, "this just ain't right."

"It's as right as it should be, Silva. And I feel better than I've felt in a very long time."

"Got to get up from here 'fore Master--"

"You just don't worry yourself about that. Worry about resting and getting better."

"And Alivia? In this house, too?"

"Aunt Sylvia, just trust me."

Sylvia didn't trust anyone when Alivia was part of it. She did not trust her memory or the woman whose bed she was laying in like she had just woken up with a new shade of skin. Mistress was the reason she was black and blue, she remembered. Then she felt Yuna was a part of this mess. Sylvia did not know how much Yuna knew or how much she did not know. It all made her head hurt even more.

The next time Sylvia woke up, it was the morning of Master Purvis' funeral.

chapter 14

NELLA JO RAN THE DISH TOWEL OVER HER hands. It was the raised skin that caught her attention and bought her back to the kitchen where she stood staring out the back door. She thought of Yuna, and the mother she had been to her. Even she knew there was a place in it all for her to have been better, but that was then. Now she was faced with an opportunity she would not let slip away. The sleepless nights since the parlor incident with Grayson had been the only thing to caress her racing mind.

It was true both Master Butler and Nella Jo had always wanted the best for their child, but it seemed for once they were in disagreement on what the best was for her now. A smile came over Nella Jo's face as she thought of Yuna wanting to teach. It was the first thing ever her daughter had taken an interest in that pleased her. There had been the need to learn to cook, how to work the loom, and even her fascination with perfect penmanship, but none had seemed good enough for Nella Jo...none good enough for *her* daughter. Maybe this teaching would turn to a fine scholarly venture. She ignored the fact that Yuna had expressed only an interest in teaching the Blacks, especially the children. Her thoughts were far ahead. In time, Yuna would outgrow such a small dream and Nella Jo would already be there, waiting and ready to welcome her into greater things. The smile hung across her face.

Then she thought of Ida, alone and weakening. She rubbed her index finger over her right wrist. The secret she'd kept from her Yuna her whole life formed scarred tissue, a worm-like raise beneath her skin. The wound had healed long ago, but the sting behind it had never subsided, not as long as Ida remained in the back of the woods.

If Master Butler had had his way and Yuna aboard a train to Philadelphia, it would only make the sting worse. It had been years since Nella Jo had said a word to Ida and even more years between then and when the words were kind and loving.

She had given her the scar.

It was Nella Jo who kept ahold of the sting each time she remembered that afternoon. The big collard leaves, rolled firm. The blade of the butcher's knife, wet with strings from the stems of the greens, clinging to its sides. The night before, Master Butler had ordered Ida to take back the evening coffee service she had brought in because it was 'weak', as he called it. She remembered the words he used as she watched Ida's bowed head from the table. It had been the first time ever Master Butler had ordered her to sit at the table as if she were his own white mistress. The whole experience seemed unreal to her, but she obeyed his instruction and took a seat. "Bring back coffee that's fit to drink and be fast about it, woman!" He was furious. Nella Jo's own heart beat against her swollen chest, full of breastmilk.

"Yes, sir, Master Butler." Ida took the tray and pushed the kitchen door open with her ample backside the way she always did. Nella Jo had known her mother to be a woman of obedience but in that instance, she saw her mother as a servant, a sad slave.

"You have to talk to her that way sometimes. She gives you looks and such as her own way of disrespecting my position. I know she's your mother, but things are changing. You'll learn to run this place better than my wife did. It's going to take some time, but you'll learn." She nodded at Master Butler's assurance. He winked an eye at her there in the parlor where just the two of them were not white master and black slave, but lovers. One an established hand over his slaves and his land, and the other, young and tender, fresh, and learning to be a First Lady within the confines of the portion of the world belonging to him. She returned a nervous smile back to him.

The next morning, Nella Jo walked into the kitchen, determined to please her dear Grayson. Mouths stopped talking and spoons stop stirring at the sight of her draped in the former Mrs. Butler's robe. She floated across the kitchen looking down a nose she was learning to hold closer towards the sky with each passing day, watching them work, spitting insulting words she had once been on the receiving end of.

"And you, sweep this flour from the floor." "Don't add so much salt to the stew." Slow, careful, and confused, they continued their work, not sure whether to obey the words coming from what was nothing more than a child lucky enough to birth their Master a baby or laugh all over themselves. For a while, they chose the latter, ringing through the kitchen in cackle and mimicking her words.

Then she came to Ida, who sliced collards with no expression of glee or misery on her face. Ignoring the laughs and taunts of the kitchen slaves behind her, she watched her mother work with diligence.

This was her moment.

This was the chance to prove to all of them, including her Grayson—especially her Grayson—she would make a suitable First Lady. She would never be laughed at again, for they would fear her and remember the day she took authority over her own mother. "And you, is that the fastest you can cut those greens. Be quicker about it, woman." The words came out of her mouth in what she thought was the same way Master Butler had said them the night before. Then, Ida had scurried off. This time, in the kitchen, at a different time of day, in a different world, something went terribly wrong. Before the last syllable of the words leaped from her mouth, Ida stood, grabbed her daughter by the arm and chopped into it with the blade. Even the strand of collard clinging to her bleeding wrist froze in its place.

She did not cry, or scream, or find words in the moment to react. She just stood, watching the blood trickle to the floor, wincing her eyes in pain. When the first tear finally fell from her eye, Samson and his limp, came into the kitchen through the back door and reached for Ida's own wrist. He snatched the knife from her hand before she could do any more harm.

The two women peered into each other for a long while before Ida broke the silence. "T'on care who you think you are today or tomorrow, you still my *child* and I am still your mother. You ain't gone talk to me any kind of way!" Just then, Master Butler entered the kitchen and the hushed room became even more still, aside from the turn of the heads in his direction and the beating of the hearts in anticipation and worry of what he was coming.

Nella Jo thought of how he ordered Ida away from the kitchen, and the main house. He moved her to the cabin she now still lived in, never to set foot in or near his house again. A few years passed before Ida laid eyes on her granddaughter again, playing in the open land. When Yuna was older, Nella Jo took her to Ida's cabin and waited outside as the granddaughter and grandchild spent time together. When it got late, she and Yuna would return to the main house, never discussing the day's time she had spent with her grandmother.

When Yuna was old enough to go on her own down into the quarters, she always made her way to her Grand Ida. The distance between Nella Jo and Yuna grew as did closeness between Ida and Yuna.

Chewy's was quiet in the late afternoon, with him outfront chopping logs when Nella Jo walked up behind him. Realizing she was there, he swung the axe into a block of wood and left it there, releasing the handle.

"Don't have nothing for you, ma'am."

"I'm not here looking for anything. Just want to know if Master Butler's been back here to talk to you about those taxes yet."

"No'm. Surprise to me ain't heard a word from him." He wiped at his forehead and headed towards the steps. "You want a drink of water?"

"I'll pass." Nella Jo looked around the grounds as if contaminated with a disease that would make her one of them, a regular black drinking regular water, in a regular place. Even still, she followed behind him up the stairs. He stopped, not wanting her to come any further. "What's the matter? I ain't welcome in that place of yours. Not even in the daytime?"

"No'm, its not that."

"Well what is it?"

"Well…"

A small boy, no more than four or five years old ran out the door of the saloon. Laughing and giggling, he leaped down the stairs, past Chewy and right into Nella Jo.

"What in the world?!"

Behind him, also past Chewy came Yuna. When she saw her mother, she stopped in her tracks, the playful smile fell from her face. The boy had backed away from Nella Jo, a tall scary statue to fear he'd been warned about.

"Mother?"

"Yuna, what's going on here?"

Yuna looked at Chewy who was sweating pellets of nervousness.

"Mother, let me explain."

"Yes, please do."

Yuna reached a hand out to Nella Jo beckoning her towards her. "Come inside."

"I most certainly will not."

"If you want to know what's going on, come inside. It's not safe to talk about it here. Now please, just come inside."

Finally, Nella Jo stepped up onto the porch into the dark place. Chewy looked away as she passed him, avoiding eye contact. The boy ran back inside past the two of them and into a back room. Outside, Chewy chopped at the wood again as Yuna explained how he was letting her use the back room a few hours in the day to work with the children. She had begun to teach them the basics she had learned at their age. It was risky and had to be kept a secret, especially now that her father had returned.

"So you really want to do this?" Nella Jo asked her daughter, seeing the joy of just talking about teaching the children put in her.

"I am doing this. I've been doing this for months."

"Months?"

"Yes, ever since little Alivia arrived here. She's Aunt Sylvia's girl. She's a smart girl. Most of these children are. They have brilliant minds, Mother. And I just can't leave here as my father wants. I know there's so much potential and so many opportunities he believes are waiting for me in Philadelphia. Oh, but Mother, I believe in the potential that's waiting for me here."

Nella Jo looked into her daughter's eyes, listened to her words. There was no way her own heart could not be affected. After a while, she smiled, sending Yuna closer to her mother. She wrapped her arms around Nella Jo's neck. The moment took her by surprise but she welcomed it, embracing her daughter in a hug they had not shared since she was a small girl.

Outside, they heard Chewy's voice, talking. They both rushed to the door and stepped out on the porch. Too late to turn around and go back inside, Master Butler turned and saw them both.

"Nella Jo? Yuna?" What's going on here? What in the world are you two doing here...in there?"

Nella Jo and Yuna looked at each other and then back at him. Yuna started, "Master..." Nella Jo raised her hand for Yuna to silence.

"Master Butler, Yuna came with me here to talk to Chewy about making sure he's keeping this place running clean and well so it brings in enough money to keep the people coming back."

"You knew about this place?"

"Of course I did."

"And you let it go on under my nose without a word. You know the kind of taxes the townsmen are leaning on me to get from this place?"

"Yes, sir. I figured having this place would be good for you to keep more of them from running off and leaving. Giving them a place like this to relax takes the taste out of their mouths of running off."

Master Butler looked at Nella Jo looking for a hole to fill her story with wrong, but there was none. She put her hand in the pocket of her dress and pulled out a roll of bills, the same bills she had been collecting from Chewy since he opened. "See, see here. This is for the taxes." He took the money from her hand and counted it. With a stern look, he eyed her, then Chewy. When his gaze landed on Yuna, his brown rose. "Yuna, what're you doing here? Is this the truth your mother telling me?" He knew Yuna would not lie to him. She adored her father just as much as he adored her.

"Yes, Father," she lied. He looked into her eyes, searching for the side of her that belonged to him. "It's exactly what she said."

He could sense the conspiracy between them, and knew it had nothing to do with Chewy, who stood with his hands at his side, fingers twitching, and sweat rolling into his eyes. Him, Nella Jo and Yuna all hoped the boy and the other children in the back would stay put while Master Butler was there. A weight sat on all of their chests, as he surveyed each of them.

"I know you're up to no good, Nella Jo. And if you insist on taking Yuna down into your mess with you, well that's fine. But, you mark my words, all three of you. If I find out there's more than you say going on here, there'll be hell to pay for each of you." He mounted his horse and turned it back towards the main house. "Nella Jo, get on back. Mrs. Butler got needs for you to tend to."

They all breathed a sigh of relief as the horse galloped away.

chapter 15

MISTRESS DID NOT MAKE a big fuss over her husband's funeral. A lot of the locals who knew him as a business person attended, but few could be called friends. The only blood relative in attendance was Mrs. Purvis and, aside from a few tears here and there, she held up pretty well for this to be the burial of her only son.

The stick Sylvia had been walking with for months dug into the palm of her hand. She leaned on it more than ever as they walked back to the main house after the service. Everyone was respectfully quiet, which only made her even more unnerved with all she did not know.

Leading the way, Mistress and Mrs. Purvis kept at a mourningful pace. It all seemed coated with a strange feeling flowing through the parade of mourners. Behind them was Master Butler and the new Mrs. Butler, a mystery of who she was and where she had come from floating through the air. Nella Jo walked directly behind the Purvis overseer and his wife silently ushered behind the Purvises. Yuna walked on one side of Sylvia, Alivia on the other. The Blacks, house workers, Master Purvis' ex-slaves, all followed between them and Julius, who hobbled behind, bringing up the rear.

That night, when Yuna returned to the cabin with Sylvia and Alivia, she handed her aunt a note from Mistress once Julius dozed off on his pallet.

"I didn't forget my promise to you, Silva."

The words disappeared from the paper as her mind knotted up under the lumps on her head. Mistress was supposed to help her family get safely to Hartha Gables, with all they needed to get started into their new lives. But if it wasn't the tea that killed her husband, as she said, why would she still hold up her end of the promise?

"Yuna." Sylvia motioned towards the door.

Outside, under a low-hanging moon, Sylvia asked questions. "And stop foolin' around with me, girl! You know more than you tellin'."

"I'm telling you what I know, Aunt Sylvia. Mistress sent for me to nurse you in her room at the main house. You were a near-dead mess. I cleaned you up and haven't left your side other than to look after Alivia and help Nan in the kitchen."

"And where was Alivia when you came for me? Oh Lord, was my babygirl hurt?"

Yuna took a moment to set a lie on her tongue, Sylvia was sure. "Aunt Sylvia, she was laying in the bed in Master's room. "

"What?"

"Shhh, Aunt Sylvia!" They were amongst sleeping-not-sleeping folk. "I did as I was told. Mistress said she didn't want the child to wake up and see you in that state. It nearly choked *me* to tears when I laid eyes on you."

Sylvia rested her hand on Yuna's shoulder. "So you don't know nothing 'bout how we got there."

"I don't." Her look became questioning, as if she was about to ask things Sylvia wouldn't know how to answer. "What's the last thing you do remember?"

"Being in the kitchen house. Holding Alivia--oh Lord, Yuna, did I really kill that white man?"

She shrugged. "I pray you didn't. But with the way you looked, you were the one who had death on you."

The next morning, Yuna took Alivia across the river to Ida's before going to the cookhouse. She barely made the walk there before having to sit. A ghost sitting on a pail, the way Nan looked at her. "Close your mouth 'fore flies get in it," Sylvia said between breaths. She kept the blade of the knife scraping against the scales of fresh herring all over the table, her eyes on Sylvia leaning on her knees.

"Don't see why you even here," Nan said, then looked at Yuna, who walked in and was tying her apron. "That child been doing your work just fine. You need to be resting."

"I tried to tell her the same thing," Yuna said, pulling down one of the small black pots.

"Neither one of ya' master over me," Sylvia rebelled. "So hush up."

"Sure ain't," Nan said and spit. "That dead white man worm food now." When Yuna and Sylvia looked at Nan, she gave them a toothless smile. "What? Well he is. Ain't no secret 'bout that."

Sylvia shook her aching head. "Nan, your mouth just say anything."

"Sure do, and I'm too old to change now. So if you waitin' on that, you got a long wait comin'."

Yuna came over and rubbed Sylvia's back. "Why don't you head over to the house and let me and Nan handle in here? Maybe Mistress or Mrs. Purvis need you to do something easy up there."

In the main house, everything was quiet. Mrs. Purvis, fully dressed with parasol in hand, standing at the top of the stairwell, called down. "Sylvia! Have the boy come around for my things. I want to get an early start before that Mercy sun ruins me."

From the front porch, Sylvia waved to the young men in the distance while Mrs. Purvis sat erect in the parlor chair, digging into her gloves.

"So soon, ma'am?" Sylvia asked once back inside.

"Well, I hardly see any need for me to stay here in Vivian's hair." She eyed the stairwell and spoke in a lower tone. "Truth be told, I think she's glad I'm not staying any longer than I am." With a slight nod, she confirmed her own words for herself.

"Sylvia, I told the boy—oh, I forget which one, they all look so alike—to put that old horse down by night's end." She sighed and took off her gloves. "Poor Early, rest his soul. The one thing he loved so much sent him to Heaven."

She put the gloves back on. "It's just so awful, Sylvia, the way something you've been so good to and provided such a good life for would turn on you like that. Quite ungrateful, that beast of a horse Creek is."

"Yes, ma'am."

"So that's the story we're telling?" Sylvia thought to herself. "Poor Creek. Poor, poor Creek. An innocent horse, carrying the load of evil on his back."

Mrs. Purvis' round-top trunk was loaded on the wagon, along with the rest of her demands. Then it was off onto the path to the normal world, where she belonged.

Yuna came in with breakfast for Mistress, who had made her way down the stairs looking paler and moving slower than usual. When she entered the dining room and saw Sylvia, she gave a smile in a way no one had ever seen—or maybe forgotten in all the years it was gone. Sylvia and Mistress watched Yuna move about setting dishes of grits and butter and smoked ham carrying an aroma that only came from food cooked by her hands. Sylvia sat the coffee pot next to Mistress.

"No, Silva. This is a morning for tea."

"Yes, ma'am." Sylvia leaned her stick against the side table to make the tea to her liking, the same way she had all these years.

"Have a seat."

Yuna stopped spooning the grits onto the plate, and Mistress' tea froze in Sylvia's hand.

"Silva, please, have a seat." She motioned towards the chair next to hers. "Yuna can handle the serving. It's fine. I want to talk with you."

The high-back chair felt strange against her shoulders, but Sylvia let her soreness lean into its cushion while doing her best to sit up straight.

"You can relax."

"Yes, ma'am." Sylvia exhaled. It was the most she knew about relaxing.

By now, Yuna had left the dining room and the two women were alone. She spoke as if in a room full of people and she was addressing each one of them.

"Arrangements have been made." She sipped her tea. "You and your family will leave in two days. That should give that husband of yours enough time to let his employer know of his travels to Hartha Gables and for you to say your goodbyes here and at Butler."

Sylvia leaned forward, relieving her back from the chair.

"There will be a driver, white, and when you arrive there, he'll give you the remainder of what was promised."

"Mistress, about Master Early--"

She placed the tea cup back in its saucer. "That will not be spoken of."

"But Mistress, I want to know--"

"Not now, not ever, Silva." Now she spoke to Sylvia as if there were other white people in the dining room, though it was only Sylvia and Yuna, who had just returned with table napkins. Mistress took one and wiped her lips, only to put the last of the smoked ham in her mouth, chew it slowly, and swallow.

"Yuna," she said with her eyes straight forward on what was now an only half-full china cabinet of crystal angels, "I am asking you to stay here, at Purvis, as my head maidservant."

Yuna looked at her aunt, waiting for approval. Her eyes begged to accept the offer, but only with Sylvia's blessings. It would be just the job she needed to help with getting money for supplies for her school. She had told her father and Mrs. Butler about her plans to teach the people of Mercy to read, write, and do match. They both sat with straight backs and stern faces, clearly unimpressed. Master

Butler, in his displeasure of her decision to not go to Philadelphia, told Yuna she would have to work for anything she needed from that point on. For the first time, he expressed his disinterest in Negros being educated. When she asked what he considered one half of her, he had called it, her 'tolerated half'. This broke her heart, thus, opening her eyes to the reality of the man who was no more than a Master to her.

When Sylvia gave a slight nod to Yuna, she exclaimed, "Yes, ma'am, I would be glad to work for you."

"Very well, then. It's settled. Silva will be heading to Hartha Gables in two days and you will take over her position here at Purvis." Yuna smiled. Sylvia smiled for her. "Also, Yuna, I would like for you to move into the downstairs room of the house. I know this transition is going to be anything but favorable to your father and that mother of yours, but I want you to be close by and have a place to go when their disapproval weighs heavy on you."

"You do?" Yuna put her hands together. "I mean, yes, ma'am! I will. At your request, Mistress."

"If there is anything you will need to settle in, let Nan know and she will assist you. I expect you will be in before Silva has left."

"Yes, ma'am!" Yuna and Sylvia sung like two birds.

"My sister will be coming to live with us very soon. I would like for you to get things ready here for her arrival." She paused to sip her tea. "And one last thing," Mistress looked Sylvia square in the eye. "Silva, you are to make sure Yuna knows how to cook fried okra exactly the way you do. It's Sister's favorite, you know."

And at the slight nod of her head, Sylvia and Yuna were permitted to laugh. Mistress couldn't help but join in. They were sure this was the first time in all the history of Mercy a white woman sat at a table with two black women and laughed like real friends.

―――●●●――――

When the afternoon sun blazed on her face Sylvia knew she was in a different place. She'd spent the majority of her life under the Mercy sun and there was something about the way it sat on the skin and melted into the pores. This Hartha Gables sun, it warmed you, but didn't cook you. It kissed you.

Julius reached over and wrapped his calloused hand around his wife's as the wagon pulled up the hill, led by Creek. Mistress had spared the horse and the two souls sitting under the covered wagon. Alivia layed in the back behind them, fast asleep on a sack of clothing.

The new city seemed enormous to Sylvia as they made it to the top of the hill. Never had she seen any place outside of Mercy her mind could remember. Men, black men, carrying logs of wood, saws and other tools back and forth in the horizon were the first things she noticed. The closer they got into the town, the clearer the picture appeared to her of a house being built. It was larger than the cabin they'd lived in on Purvis. Julius, in rare form, leaned over and whispered into Sylvia's ear. "That there is where we gone live real soon." The large frame of the house seemed too much for them. Their family was just the three of them. She was sure they would live there with others. Continuing further, past their future house, were several other houses. They were all the same size as the one Julius pointed out. Or bigger. Her mind couldn't make sense of what she was seeing.

The wagon pulled in front of what looked and smelled like a house built not too long ago. The smell of pine lingered in the air as they stepped down off the wagon. Out the front door came a woman, a negro woman, carrying a baby in her arms. The entire scene seemed awkward to Sylvia.

"Well look like y'all made it in one piece!" she yelled, excited. Sylvia smiled but had no idea who the woman was. Then from the same door, out came a man who Sylvia assumed to be the woman's husband. Julius stepped onto the porch and embraced him in a familiar way. The man placed a straw hat on his head. It covered his eyes and the shade of the hat's rim veiled most of his face.

"Come on. Come on." Julius motioned Sylvia up the steps and onto the porch. "They don't bite." He laughed.

"This here is my wife, Sylvia." Julius said to the man. Sylvia, this here is Opal, Fedil's wife." In that instant, Alivia rushed past her, past Julius and hugged the woman with every ounce of life in her. Sylvia didn't know what to make of it. Then the name hit her and it made sense. Opal. Fedil. They were the ones Alivia had told her were her mother and father. As sadness came over Sylvia, a feeling of being lost, but she held herself together and smiled at the reunion.

"Well, guess we don't need to tell ya' who that one is." Julius laughed. Sylvia had forgotten his laugh. It was hearty and full. She couldn't resist the slight smile coming over her face.

"Well come on in. Sun still get hot here too," Opal said as she led them inside. Alivia followed close behind her mother. The men headed back down the steps to unload the wagon of the few belongings they had bought with them.

"Ma'am." It took Sylvia a moment to realize the driver was calling out to her. She walked over to him. While Julius and Fedil laughed and talked like old friends at the back of the wagon, the white driver handed her a book. It was a Bible with gold trim around the pages, and letters much larger than the old torn sheets she had held on to. She flipped through the pages just to feel them on her fingers and there she saw the stack of bills. Sylvia had never seen such an amount of money in all of her life. A coin here and there, maybe two or three to jangle in her hand when she went to town with Mistress for errands, but never bills. "From Mrs. Purvis."

"Thank you. Thank you kindly."

"Where would you like the horse?"

"I beg your pardon?"

"The one in front. I've been instructed to leave that one with you."

"With me? Creek staying here?"

Just then Julius came around the side of the wagon, still wearing a smile as high as his pants tucked around him. "Well glory be! That's what the man said. I'll take him 'round back. That white lady sho' is somethin' else. We thank her, kindly."

"Yes, yes." Sylvia shut the bible, hiding it and the bills beneath the shawl Mistress had wrapped around her shoulders the night they left. "Please tell her thank you for us when you return." Sylvia's eyes watered. Mistress had not only kept her promise but spared Creek against Mrs. Purvis' orders and sent him along to a new life with she and Julius.

"Oh stop all that and get on inside with Opal and the youngins." Julius slapped her backside and sent her on. This, indeed, was a new life.

Later that evening, the table was lined with fried chicken parts, biscuits, beans, and potatoes. Fedil sat at one end of the hand-carved table he had made himself, while Julius was at the other. There was enough room for Opal, Alivia, Sylvia and a few more people. It felt strange. She felt out of place. To simply place the plate of biscuits did not soothe her feelings of needing to get up and serve everyone and stand against the kitchen door, within earshot of any sudden request for more tea, or a second helping of potatoes. She shifted in her chair trying to find a place on the smooth seat fitting for her discomfort. Halfway through the dinner, she realized, there just was not such a place. After dinner, Sylvia rose to clear the table and begin the dishes. It wasn't until then she felt the slightest bit of familiarity in the new place she was expected to call home. Opal and Alivia chatted as she stood silently drying the bowls and cups. When all the dishes were put away, they were shown to their bedrooms. She felt awkward in a room with a door. It silenced the sounds of the remainder of the house. Alivia was in another room, Opal tucking her daughter—no longer Sylvia's —in to sleep with a kiss and a prayer the way Sylvia had done since she had come to her. Seeing the gesture brought a sadness she didn't know how to identify.

"You hardly said two words since we step off the wagon." Julius said pulling his worn shoes off of swollen feet. The bed was higher off of the ground than their straw stuffed sacks they were accustomed to. He leaned a hand over to what was Sylvia's side of the bed to help pull her up.

"Don't really got nothin' to say."

"You happy here?"

"Julius," Sylvia untied the scarf around her head and folded it. "We ain't been here a day. I can't tell you if I'm happy here. I'm barely here." Her response and the slight smile she gave must not have set well with him. His face looked grave. His eye twitched in the way it usually did when he was starting to get upset. The last thing she wanted was to be embarrassed by a beating on the first night in this place. She had to think of something to soothe him. "I love that we have a door on our room." He didn't respond. This made her even more nervous. She turned to get off of the bed and walk over to the door. She wanted to point out the woodwork to him and maybe even suggest that she thought he could do this kind of work with no problem because he was such a skilled man. But, before she could fully leave the bed, the same hand he extended to help her up wrapped around her wrist so tight she could feel the stopping of blood attempting to circulate into her hand.

"You gone find a way to be happy here." He spoke through a clenched jaw and eyes that peered straight ahead. "You best find yourself here, cause this is home from now on. We gone be here for a long while so you betta make do. You hear me?"

She nodded without taking her eyes off of the door where she had glued them. Funny how the one thing she took a liking to about being in Hartha Gables was the one thing she now feared sealed her inside the room along with any cry for help she would ever make when Julius' temper flared.

The house had two rooms, a kitchen with a small potbelly stove, and a place out front and back for two separate gardens. This excited Sylvia most about their new house. There were so many windows, one in every room. For weeks, as she worked to turn the house into a home for her and Julius, arranging what few belongings they had brought with them from Mercy, she stopped at every window, in every room and admired the different views. From the bedroom, she could see the moon at night. It sat in such a way it lit the room and most times, there was no need for a candle or lamp. Nothing else about it felt much like a home to her at all. Just big, with too many rooms to remind her of who was not there. There were no sons and no daughters, and no Alivia, to fill the space. Alivia had stayed with her family, up under Opal's every move. When she saw the two of them together, at times, it tore Sylvia's heart to watch. Alivia now followed behind her mother the way she had with Sylvia just a few months ago.

The sun cast a blanket of afternoon warmth on her back as she dug into the dirt. Cool to her fingers, she did not mind the way the earth caked itself beneath her nails. Sylvia had become so used to looking up and seeing Alivia's face across from her when she worked her herb garden back in Mercy.

"Don't know why you putting them kind of flowers out here. And so many of 'em. Got plenty room in the other garden out back." He dropped some of the seeds he was holding for her into her raised hand.

"Julius, these here are Bitter Buttons. They gone make pretty yellow flowers and give us a lil color out here. 'Sides, this closer to the front door. Keep the moths out the house." She laughed a bit, not too much to disturb his manhood, but just enough to remind him she had been working a garden her entire life and knew it as good as she knew his next move. Sylvia caught the smile on his face, looking down at her patting the soil. Her Junebug was still a handsome man when his eyes did not bulge with anger. She always knew it was the shackle of being who he was and having to live the life he was given that made him hurt. It was what made him hurt her. The man helping her get her herbs and flowers started at the new place they were calling home was the man Sylvia loved a little bit more than the man who knocked her around.

"So what you gone put over here?" Both of them looked in the direction he pointed while she dug the backs of her wrists into her sides and stretched straightness into her back. "How 'bout some of them prickly things."

This time Sylvia couldn't hold back her laugh. "Julius, what prickly things you talkin' 'bout?"

"Like you had long time ago."

"You gone have to tell me more than that for me to know what you talkin' 'bout." She got up from the ground, leaning in on one knee and digging her walking stick into the ground. It took her by surprise when Julius' outstretched hand dangled in front of her. She looked him in his eyes before reaching for it. It took a moment to remember this man and tell herself she could trust him, even if just for the moment.

Inside, they both sipped tea from the jars they drank from everytime thirst arose. No words passed between them as they watched the breeze battle with the half hung curtain Sylvia had strung over the open window. It was the same curtain she had had at her old cabin. Opal teased about it being time for new things, bringing over a curtain she made for Sylvia with too many of colors in it. Sylvia hung Opal's curtain to the back window, but in the front, where she looked out at the world, Sylvia put her old one up. It was one of the few familiar things left in her life she could not abandon or have taken away.

Passing the window, Sylvia saw Opal's headscarf go by. She came up on the porch with an armful of cloth in more wild patterns and colors. Sylvia left the wooden chair Julius had made for her years ago and met Opal outside.

"I can't believe you got that old thing still hanging in your window." Opal laughed, handing her a folded paper. It was a letter. Sylvia looked back at the door and then gave her new friend a cautious eye. Understanding, Opal slid the letter back into her apron pocket for later. "It still work." They both gave a strained laugh, shaking off the awkwardness of the moment. "How's my babygirl doing today?"

"She got a cough, Ms. Sylvia. Woke up with it. But she gone be just fine."

"It's dead of spring, too nice for a cold." Sylvia said, again, looking back to make sure Julius was staying put in his chair. Speaking a bit louder so he could hear her through the open door and window, "Maybe I'll hobble on over with you and see what I can do to get her up and feeling better." Pulling the door shut, she saw Julius had already dozed off in the cool breeze.

Getting up the hill was becoming more difficult for her with each visit. Opal took notice of Sylvia's labored breathing and slowed her pace, slipping the paper from her apron again when they were out of eye's distance of a sleeping Julius. The letter was from Yuna. She pressed it to her nose just to get the smell of familiar. When they reached the top of the hill, Opal went on ahead, leaving her to her moment.

Dear Aunt Sylvia,

I pray this letter reaches you in the best of time in your new life and new home. Has Hartha Gables been good to you? I know it has taken me a while to write, but Mistress warned it would be most wise if we waited for a bit of time to pass before contacting you.

A letter came from Mrs. Puvis stating she will not be visiting again, ever. Mistress nearly lost her bosom in her laughter and joy of the message. I guess the thought of never having to see the one person who makes her shiver would indeed be a great delight.

Oh Aunt Sylvia, I do pray the new life you are living is all you dreamed it would be. Know that you are missed dearly.

All my love,
Yuna

Alivia layed in her bed, beads of sweat covering her forehead, sick indeed. Sylvia may not have been her mother, but she knew this was much more than a cough. Rushing past Opal, back down the hill to her own house as fast as her feet and walking stick would take her, she grabbed her jar of herbs. By the time she returned, Opal was finished heating water as instructed. Sylvia told her to bring in a cup so she could prepare tea.

"You gotta drink this for me, Livy." She held the cup to her lips and like her eyes, they barely parted. Opal stood in the doorway, trusting Sylvia's wisdom and remedy. Sylvia, glad for the moment to hold Alivia close, rocked her back to sleep.

Hours later, the fever broke leaving the child with a hearty appetite. Opal prepared a broth and within minutes, Alivia drank every bit of it.

Night was coming and Sylvia headed back before Julius' stomach rumbled.

"You come down and get me if she turn back, you hear me? Don't matter 'bout the time or nothing else, just come." She winked at Alivia's strengthening smile.

"Thank you, Ms. Sylvia."

"Thank you, Ma Syl." The words were strong enough to send Sylvia down the hill with her walking stick tucked beneath her arm, unneeded.

On the front porch of the house, she savored the girl's words and admired the sunset before heading in, realizing Julius was watching her from the doorway of the kitchen. "You hungry?" She moved towards the kitchen, easing through the small space he left for her to pass him.

"What you think? You been out there messin' around all day. Where you been?"

Sylvia rustled with the pots and pans, trying to keep the tremble starting in her hands under enough control to keep them steady.

"Livy took sick. I made her up some tea and sat with her 'til she come 'round."

"Sylvia, you ain't that girl momma."

Before she realized it, her own temper flared. "Don't you think I know that, Julius." She slammed the pot on the table. "If I don't know nothing, I know what ain't mine to have and keep." Her voice cracked with the words she spoke, and tears gathered in her eyes. She blinked and swallowed.

They ate together in silence. His brewing temper simmered somewhere in her response and fried fat back and biscuits with gravy.

"What else she give you?" He broke the silence.

"What you talking 'bout?" Sylvia placed the last of her biscuit in her mouth and ran her crooked finger through the gravy, sucking at it.

"Mistress. What else she give you?"

She cleared away the dinner, his tone worrying at her nerves. She kept the money hidden in the big bible, safe from Julius. It was her promise to herself if she ever had to make it on her own, she would use the money then and only then. There was no way she would let Julius take that away from her too. She earned it and it was hers.

"Last thing you gone do is sit here and act like I'm some kinda fool. We get here safe wit' not a lick'a trouble on da same path White folk killing us like flies. Get here an' got food and ev'ything else ready fo' us. I'm barely doin' work. This town new, ain't free. So 'fore you fix yo' mouth up for lying, you think 'bout what answer you gone give me." Sylvia watched him out the corner of her eye flexing his own fingers flat on the table, then in a ball, then flat again.

The truth came out of her mouth. "Mistress help us, yes. She help me cause I done made life comfortable, bearable, for her all these years. We like friends."

"You black, she white. You ain't no friends, Sylvia." His voice roared. "What else?"

"Nothin' else."

"What else?!"

"Julius, I don't know what you want me to say." He rose from the table and came up behind her. "I already tell you she helped."

"I hear you tell me that, but what I wanna know is the part you ain't telling me."

An image of Master Purvis standing in rage in the kitchen house the same way Julius was standing in their kitchen flashed through her mind. She wanted to cry, but knew it would not do anything for her. Tears would not answer his questions and it would not stop the heat of his breath burning into her neck.

To her surprise, he stepped back and walked out the kitchen. She expected to be flat on the floor. When she heard the front door close behind him, she let herself breathe. She had no idea what had gotten him off of her back, but she was thankful. The next time he came at her with those questions—and she knew there would be a next time —she needed to know what her answers would be.

Sleep came easy once she dried the last of the dishes and laid down. In her dream, she found herself walking through town. The post office to the left side of her with door lit up in such a way, she could not help walking towards it. Inside, mounds of unopened letters covered the floors and counters, all addressed to her. Desperate to know the answers to the many questions running around in her mind, she tore through them, finding only bits and pieces of body parts inside each envelope. In one, an ear. In another, a white man's finger with a gold wedding band. And still in another, a bulging eyeball. Tossing aside the envelopes in terror and desperation, she rushed through the piles opening one after the other. The door, slamming shut and then open several times, calling her attention from her madness, revealed Alivia's lit silhouette. She hesitated when the child motioned for her to follow. When she did, the closer she got to her babygirl, the further away Alivia floated, leading them out into center of Hartha Gables. By now, it was pitch dark, with a sky filled with more than one moon. There were four, each casting a white light on the brick road where they stood. Alivia stood still as Sylvia moved closer to her. When she was close enough to make out her face, she gasped. Alivia carried the facial features of Master Purvis, yet the body of her sweet child. "What happened? Tell me what happened to Master Purvis', Livy?" Sylvia shouted desperately. "What happened?!?!" Each time the question left her lips, the light of the moons dimmed and everything became darker until she could no longer see the face, only sensing Alivia was still standing in front of her. "What happened?" She asked a final time, on her knees, sobbing.

Then Sylvia woke up, beads of sweat stinging her eyes and drenching her nightgown. Beside her, Julius kicked at her legs in his own nightmares.

chapter 16

THE BACON SMELL LINGERED in the kitchen when Yuna came through the back door. For a short moment, she stopped in her steps when she realized it was her mother cooking.

"Oh don't look at me like that. I do know how to cook."

"You sure do. It smells good in here." Yuna smiled, watching her mother plate the food. "Where is everyone?"

"Everyone like who?"

"The servants."

"Oh, well Master Butler is gone into town and Mrs. said she didnt feel up to eating this morning, so I sent them all away. Gave them the day off."

"And what about lunch and dinner? What if they…"

"Yuna, it'll be fine."

Nella Jo could feel the confused look her daughter gave her as she scooped the hot grits into a bowl. "This is for somebody else."

"Should I ask who?"

"No you shouldn't." They both laughed. "Besides, what you doing here this morning? You alright? How things going over on Purvis?"

"Fairly well, actually. I do believe Ms. Sister is starting to come around now that she's out of that place and at home with Mistress. Her hair is even growing back in. Its amazing, Mother. The power of being with the only family she knows is bringing her back to her old self again." Yuna beamed with excitement for Mistress and her sister. Nella Jo placed the few strips of bacon on the plate with a smile of her own, understanding all too well what her daughter spoke about. "I just hate that I've been so busy, I haven't had the time to get over to Grand Ida's as much as I'd like."

"I'm sure she's fine."

Yuna ignored her mother's assumed certainty. She needed to know how fine her grandmother was for herself, but between working with the children over at Chewy's and caring for Mistress and Ms. Sister, she was wearing away.

Nella Jo enjoyed the morning, the kind she dreamed of since Yuna was a child. After a bit more chat between them, a child came to the backdoor with wild and fuzzy braids calling for her. Yuna rushed off back.

Nella Jo held the hem of her dress as she headed down into the quarters, with her boots, once meaning the world to her, leading the way. The feel of the gravel beneath her feet made her a bit unsteady, holding the covered plate in her hands. She took a moment to breathe her way through her walk and the thoughts going through her mind.

In the distance, she could see children playing, a girl and a boy. There was no way to avoid the rush of emotions shivering through her body as she saw herself in the face of the girl. The Nella Jo she had been back then, an innocent child before Grayson, before Yuna, when she was Julius' sister and playmate, stood before her. She hid behind the big tree, waiting to be found. Patient and still, the girl held the hem of her dress the same way Nella Jo did just moments earlier. The child, hiding, noticed Nella Jo and froze. Not in play, but in fright. She had been taught to fear the woman known as First Lady. It was her mother who told her to watch out for the ways of such a person, just as Ida had warned her own daughter about White folk. They were not to be trusted, not to be looked away from for not knowing what they would do. It was in the girl's eyes Nella Jo feared her own self and the person she had become.

Long ago were the times when she was able to look into the water and love the reflection staring back at her. So far away was the person she once was, innocent and loving, the way her mother had taught her to be. Was it in the arms of love she lost herself? When she dropped the veil and became First Lady of Butler plantation, she had lost Nella Jo, the woman. So much had been given up to become what she thought she wanted to be.

"Get here!" A mother scurried her daughter away from the tree and into their cabin leaving behind a sadness and confusion to dangle from the girl to Nella Jo like a web. "Mornin' ma'am. Mornin'." Even the mother's eyes were colored in pure terror of being before her. A single tear layed on the rim of Nella Jo's eyelid.

The boy, fearless, or simply rebellious refused to go inside, ignoring his mother's call. He reminded her of Julius. He was younger than her but had been a source of protection for her. She remembered the night the two of them, twelve and eight years old, made promises life would never allow them to keep.

"I'm gonna take care of you. And you take care of Mother."

"Julius you just a boy, you can't stand up to no white man."

"But I can run. I can run real fast, Nella Jo. You seen me run ya'self. Anybody mess wit' you, I'll get them and be gone, running like lightening in the sky."

Julius ran. He ran time and time again, leaving Nella Jo behind. After so many times, her heart hardened to her only brother. He had been the first of men in her life to leave her behind. She was left to fight her own battles, protect herself. Even the day the man with the tunnel between his teeth pinned her to the ground by the chicken coop, gagging her to silence with his handkercheif, and planting his unwanted seed inside her while Grayson was away. Julius did not protect her, not then, not ever. And she dared not tell Grayson as it would be her word against a white man's...a townsman with influence. So she never told him, never wanting to break his heart and make him choose between her and the world. She was just thankful her final months of carrying the seed coincided with his next trip away. She was able to maintain her position of his First Lady, beneath heavy winter clothing and a secret tucked away from everyone.

Grayson once made her feel what she now knew to be falsities. His love had been worth the lies and the loss. Now, in a different state of mind, standing near the same tree Julius hugged all those years ago, she knew better. Nella Jo could hear the crack of the whip breaking into skin, ripping flesh from flesh, brother from sister, mother from child. While she had stood there, in terror and pain for both her mother and brother, she was the one to walk away into a life of new promises and guarantees. She thought then Grayson loved her. In fact, Grayson was love to her. When in truth, he had made her even more of a slave, the worse kind of slave—the kind that does not realize they are a slave. He had taken away her family and her people and turned her against them. In her loss, he had stolen her daughter's heart, giving his to her until she became a woman with her own desires that did not include his welfare. He had made her believe she was more than other slaves, when in fact, she was less, because she had been left with nothing but fancy bows, lilac oil and a silver buckled pair of boots.

Nella Jo looked down at her feet, planted on the same path connecting her to then and now. The boy was now gone, having left while she was preoccupied with her thoughts. She continued through the quarters, turning corners and finding her way back to Ida's.

Outside the cabin, the leaves piled across the porch. The seasons were changing and with all the work Yuna had on her plate, there had been no time to sweep. Just beside the door was Ida's broom, the same one Nella Jo remembered using as a child. She placed the plate on the corner of the porch where the boards met and took the broom in her hand. With a breath, she began sweeping away the leaves as though they were the years she had lost, abandoned.

"Yuna? Tha's you?" Ida called from inside. Nella Jo, not wanting to disappoint Ida that she was not the granddaughter she hoped for sweeping her porch, said nothing. She was also still wrestling with the words in her head she came to say. "Yuna?"

When Ida did not get a response, Nella Jo could heard her mother raising from the chair inside, her feet shuffling in small steps towards the door.

"What you doing here? And why you sweeping my porch?" Ida chewed at her toothless gums. It had been years since the two of them had been so close in each other's presence. Nella Jo, there, but still unsure of how ready she was to face the mother she'd betrayed and denied for so long, continued to sweep.

"You hear me?" Ida asked her. "You done gone all the way crazy? Nella Jo?"

Finally, she stopped sweeping and turned to the half open door with the feeble body facing her. "No. I mean, no ma'am."

"No ma'am?" Ida scrunched her nose. "What done got into you? And why in the devil is you back here sweeping?"

"Mother..." The word vanished into the autumn air. "Mother..." She tried again, but nothing followed.

"Mother? Oh that's who I am now?"

"You never stopped. I just stopped being your daughter."

"Had better things to do being First Woman or whatever you callin' yourself."

"I call myself Nella Jo." She placed the broom against the wall and headed over to the plate of food. "That's the name you gave me."

She held the plate of food towards Ida. Ida looked at the covered plate suspicious, then back at her daughter. "What's that?"

"Food. Breakfast."

"Who made it?"

"I did."

Ida stretched her thin brows to the sky, then grunted. "Got poison in it?"

"Mother..." Then she realized Ida wore a smile on her face. The same warm smile she remembered comforting her long ago the way a mother comforted her child. It was not until then she felt the cord linking them together, chopped by both her and Ida, begin to mend.

"Well bring it on in here and let me see if ya still know your way round that kitchen like I taught ya."

chapter 17

SUMMER CAME TO AN END leaving those with small farms calling for the help of those who didn't to help with the crops. The same went for those who owned boats and went out into the waters for fish and other foods. Everyone needed some kind of help and they all pulled together to get it done. Sylvia and Opal worked with many of the nearby farm women pulling in vegetables, cleaning, canning and whatever else needed to be done. The men, every morning, made their way to the docks and pulled in shrimp nets filled with shrimp, crabs, and whatever else came up. Both food and work were plentiful.

"I'll see you tonight, pretty lady." Julius beamed as he headed to the water with the other men of Hartha Gables, lunch in his sack. His walk, even with a limp was lively and so full of purpose, Sylvia couldn't deny the smile settling into her own face as she watched him walk away. He waved a hand with swollen joints and broken skin until he disappeared into the town.

She'd only been back inside a moment before Alivia and Opal came through the door with the baby tied to her front the way women did when they headed to the fields. For a short moment, she pictured Opal as herself and her baby as her son. Any of them. The youngest one pulled at her hair with chubby hands. One eye milky, but she never doubted he could see her love for him just fine, even up to the day she handed him over.

She caught herself lost in the baby's wide eyes.

"I don't think he gone give us a fuss today. Been cooing all morning and finding his toes."

"Oh he ain't never no trouble by my say," Sylvia pulled the door shut behind her as they headed over to the farm.

It was a good day. By the time it came to an end, she was as tired as a workday in the cookhouse. The owners of the farm they worked sent them home with a sack of potatoes, and several bushels of corn. It took everything in the two women to get up the hill with the food and the children. Once they settled inside, she put on water for tea.

"Your garden coming along nice. It still keep in the fall and winter?"

"Sure enough. But, I got enough herbs dried already to last me past then. The rest of 'em still coming up, like it don't know the weather changing. Guess I'll take the rest to town and see 'bout selling 'em at the store."

"Now that's a good idea. You should make some of your own blends. Give 'em a fancy name and all." They laughed at the thought , though it stuck with Sylvia through the night as she made dinner, listened to Julius go on about the fish he'd caught, and drifted off into sleep. The next morning when Opal showed up, she found Sylvia working her garden out back. "Ain't goin' today. Got fancy tea blends to make." She winked at Alivia, who seemed to be getting taller by the day. Sylvia popped off a sprig of spearmint and handed it to her. The girl crinkled her nose as she sucked at the leaf. Opal smiled at her friend and headed down the hill for work.

The garden hummed. Sylvia swore she could hear the unfolding of blossoms of purple coneflower. It was a new herb for her. Mistress had read about it in one of her many books and sent off for seeds in a catalogue. She gave them to her as a gift wrapped in a piece of silk the night before she left Mercy. When she asked Opal if she knew anything about them she told her the only thing she know was they had some sort of medicine powers. For Sylvia, that was enough. It was all she needed to know. Herbs healed the body and that was what fascinated her about them. So she welcomed the seeds in the soil when she planted them and asked the moon to give them the great power to heal whatever part of the body they were sent to work on. Now, the petals were reaching outward for the sun, ready.

By mid morning, the sun was at full blast, sending her to the porch for cool shade. Everything felt hushed as the neighbors were all somewhere doing something for one another. The thought brought a smile over her as she rested her eyes and laid her head against the back of the chair. Before long, she was awakened by the sound of Julius dragging his feet across the porch, past her, into the house.

"What's wrong? What's the matter?" She asked following him inside. "What'chu doin' home already?"

"Damn fools don't know a thing about working a net." He leaned back in his chair a moment, then, as if called by name, jumped forward and lunged at his own foot. He struggled with it, twisting back and forth trying to get his shoe off.

"Let me help you with that." Sylvia lowered to her knees. Julius moved around in a fit, flinging his foot like a mad man. "Hold still, will…." before the words made it out of her mouth, Julius' wailing foot kicked right into Sylvia's face and she toppled over on the floor. "Julius." The voice making its way out of her was defeated and worn.

"Get up from there and help me, will ya!" He barked as she watched him still struggling with the heel, blind to her sprawled out on the floor in front of him. By the time she was back up to her knees, he screamed out in pain. The shoe peeled from his swollen foot, taking the skin of his heel with it.

"Good Lord, Julius!" He looked relieved to have shoe was off, even with the sight of the raw skin staring at them, blistered and raw. Again, he laid his head back against the chair. "Let me get some water on."

When she came back with the hot water and herbs to soak his foot, he had already dozed off. She left him and his foot alone for the rest of the day.

A week went by and his foot grew worse with scabs and pussing. She tried every herb ritual she knew and those offered by neighboring women. Nothing worked. The infection spread more and started to eat away at his leg. After a while, they both needed a walking stick to get around.

With an infection eating away at him, his helplessness took him to new heights of madness and irritation. She was thankful his strength, though, could not meet his temper. He had not hit her once in the months they lived in Hartha Gables. Though, there were times in the past days he ailed so much, the sting of his words hurt her to her core. He said things he knew would hurt her worse than his hand across her face.

Her sons.

Their sons. He teased, a painful and meaningless tease, of their boys not knowing she even existed, content in the bosom of their new mothers. One night, in a dripping sweat, hanging half off the side of the bed, he swore at her and told her if any of their sons were still alive, they probably hated her and did not care if she were dead or alive.

On the porch, Sylvia sobbed into the moonlight. She knew his words were nothing more than anger towards his helplessness. Even still, she could not help letting the hurtful thoughts play through her mind. What if the cruel words Julius screamed from an angry, foaming mouth, were indeed true? What if there was a bit of truth of her sons not caring about her? What if they did not even know of her? Her heart broke at the thought of maybe, just maybe, they knew another as their mother. They lived in a time where mothers were the ones who reared you, not the one who birthed you.

Sylvia thought of Alivia, tears welling in her eyes. In a place and time where freedom was supposed to be hers, she felt robbed. Her children had been taken away. Alivia, though she never truly belonged to Sylvia, had been given back to the ones she belonged to from the start. And then there was Julius, a soul buried beneath so much fury and hatred, he was taken from her long before he was ever truly hers. But she loved the man who screamed her name from the back room. She dried her face on the hem of her dress and headed back inside, carrying her heavy heart.

He continued barking at her, favoring a manged dog with his panting between his insults. With each word, she boiled in all she festered in the years of being married to him. She could have taken the blade right out of the tin can and slit his throat across the big vein bulging from his sweat drenched neck. She could have watched the blood flow out of him and soak the sheets from a dingy white to a crimson red. If Sylvia really had it in her, and she believed she did, she could kill him tonight and be long gone with the bible and money by morning.

But she could not.

Where would she go? All she knew was Mercy. She did not even know the land between Hartha Gables and the way back. As much as Hartha Gables resembled the dream place everyone talked about, it was still a foreign land for her. There was so much new going on around her, new home, new freedom.

"Get me a drink." Julius ordered through near death sickness. His words crawled out of his throat wrapped in hoarseness and bearing no strength. Sylvia put the tin cup to his lips with her hand behind his head so he could sip. He drank with slow, fragmented gulps, raising his hand a bit when he was done. She released his head back down and his breathing quickened with the slight exertion. Still, he never opened his eyes.

Sylvia looked around the room, the same way she had a million times in the nights they had been laid out on the floor. Whatever had ahold of him made him weak, but his attitude was still one of the man who would drag her across floors. Now he was at her mercy. No one to care for him but her. It was her duty as a wife and she did not know if she would have done it for any other reason. She had to admit, there was a certain bit of delight in watching him suffer. For the past few nights, she did her share of praying for forgiveness about thinking such thoughts. But in the daylight, when the sun charged through the window and burned at his feverish body, she smiled when his eyes were closed.

"You hungry, Julius?" She asked, standing to stretch her legs.

"No."

"You haven't eaten since morning. And you didn't even keep that down." She rotated her neck in its socket before taking up the cup Julius had drank from all day. It needed to be washed, and by the smell of the room, she could use a bath, too.

"Food and water."

"That's what you want?"

"That's what you is."

"Hush now." She dabbed the sweat on his forehead. "Fever got you talking crazy."

"I know good and well what I'm sayin'." His words slowed with his breathing, calming for the first time in days. As happy as Sylvia was for the break, there was a strangeness about it. "I'm saying what I've got to say and you gone listen." He coughed up mucus and spit it on the floor next to the bed with no regard.

"Rest Julius."

"Don't tell me to rest! Don't tell me to..." He got his self worked up and started breathing heavy again. She rubbed a salve on his wet chest. He caught a weak hold of her hand. "You ain't dumb. Ain't never been." His breathing slowed again. "It's a lot you think I don't know. You think I ain't smart enough for nothing but working and drinking. And maybe I ain't. But I know you reads." Her eyes stretched. "You read them pages you got hid in that mattress. Even know'd one time you hid 'em down in the roots of your garden back in Mercy."

"Well Julius." By the time the words left her mouth she realized she didn't have anything to say after them. They both sat in silence for a while.

"Don't matter now no how." He coughed again. It took a while to get himself together but when he did, he continued. "And I know more things. Things you wanna know Sylvia." Hearing her name on his tongue felt the way it had many years ago, but she not dared let the feeling get too close. Nothing so good ever lasted. "Sylvia, you wanna know about Massah Purvis…'bout what happen to him."

She did, but there was a part of her that had settled inside with not knowing. The last place she figured any kind of explanation would come from would be Julius. Again, she patted the rag against his head and neck.

"Sure right I wanna know. But ain't been at the front of my mind since you took sick. All I been focused on was taking care of you. Ain't much left of me, Julius."

"Same for me."

"What you mean?"

"I took care of you." He took as much of a deep breath as his congested chest allowed. "When I came looking for you and saw him standing over your body, first thing come in my mind was you was dead and this white man done kill you."

"Julius!"

"Hush now and just listen."

"You ain't telling me you the one kill Master Purvis, is you? I know you ain't telling me that!" She stood to her feet, backing away from a man who had been more than a perfect stranger in all the years she believed she knew him. "Tell me, Julius. You tell me right now!"

"I can't tell you that." He gasped a bit for air. "A lot of things I done did in this life of mine likely ain't gone get me into that Heaven you talk about. But I ain't gone add one more lie to it. If this my last chance to do right, then this gone be it." He ran his tongue over his dry lips. "I'm telling you I couldn't stop myself when I see of both you and that child laying there on that kitchen floor. It may not be right what I done, but I done it."

Every tear left in her came pouring from Sylvia's eyes. "All the times you knocked me on the floor…"

"One thing I know is all I ever done came from a mixin' of what White folk showed me was the way to handle you and all the fire they put in me doin' them same things to me." Another coughing fit. "When I saw you hurt by somebody else hand, my mind went crazy."

"Julius, you killed somebody. You done a lot of wrong by me in our time, but kill somebody? I can't…I just don't…"

"What should I'a done, Sylvia?! What a man 'posed to do he see his wife looking dead and a white man, same man order me whipped more times than I can remember standin' over you with the tip of his shoes at yo' head. That child you love on so much layin' flat on the ground 'cross from you. What I was gone do, huh? You tell me?"

"I don't know!" Sylvia screamed throwing her hands to the Heavens. "I just don't know. It's just the times we living in. White folk beat Black folk. Men beat on women. Just how it is. I 'cept it long time ago."

"Maybe so, but I've taken more than my share of beatings and ain't a doubt in my mind I gave you more than yours." He let out a sigh. His breath shaking the flame in the lamp she set beside the bed when night came. "It just happened."

"What I wanna know is…"

"That's it, Sylvia. Thats it."

"That can't be it.You done kill a white man. And not just any ol' white man. We talking about one of Mercy's finest. How his own White wife telling a story covering your tracks? Why she ain't got you strung up hanging from a tree long before his body got cold? You tell me that, Julius."

"I said that's it." He turned his back to Sylvia. "That's all I got to say about it."

She watched the cover over his shoulder rise and fall with his breathing. His answer to her question only fueled a million more. He was drifting to sleep while she went back and forth in her mind on whether she should ask for more than he had already given. Sylvia wondered if she could even handle knowing anymore. "How you do it Julius? Just tell me that." He never answered, awake or in the sleep he drifted to.

The next day, Julius barely woke. He slept through all phases of morning, noon, and into the late evening, barely eating the lemongrass soup or the bread. Sylvia was exhausted. It had been weeks since she herself had gotten a full night's sleep. Every since his heel came off in his shoe and his rants were even more unpredictable, she stayed on edge…on guard. Awake and ready for anything.

Outside under the night sky, the many stars were present. Sylvia set up the big tub with a long cloth to use as a towel on the ground. She welcomed the hot water, releasing steam into the night, while she undressed and stepped into the tub. She could feel every bone in her body thank her for the soothing water. Her knees, bent into the tub kissed the water in gratitude. Once she situated her body, laying her legs across the side of the tub, she let the breezeless night have its way with her thoughts as she dozed off.

Sylvia was awakened by the sound of glass breaking. Startled, she leaped from the tub and threw her dress over her head. Again, another sound of glass breaking. Then, as her eyes focused and her mind sorted itself out, she saw it. The flames of fury fire bursting through the back window of the house. For a moment, she froze, unable to believe what was happening. Grabbing her dress, she ran to the front of the house, hoping the fire had not made its way there.

Julius was inside.

He was sick with not enough strength to get up from where he laid for too long.

Just as she reached the front of the house, she was met by Opal. "Oh God! Are you okay?" Just as the words came from her mouth, another sound of broken glass burst through the side window. "I'm fine, but Julius..." Sylvia sobbed. "Julius in there. We gotta help him!" Opal grabbed Sylvia's arm and pulled her back from the house where she tried to charge up onto the porch. She struggled to get away, she needed to save her husband.

"You can't go in there. We gotta get back, Sylvia." Then Fedil came running towards them, along with three other men from nearby houses. One of them carried a pail of water.

"Where's Julius?" Sylvia could not answer, still struggling to loosen herself from Opal's grip. "Oh Lord." Realizing Julius was inside, he dashed over to the other men, and told them there was someone inside the house. Sylvia pointed to the back of the house where she had left the tub of bathwater. One of the men followed her pointing hand and found it, dousing it through the broken back windows. The other men worked to drench the house with the pails of water brought by wives and others neighbors realizing what was happening. Fedil kicked at the front door and tossed a pail of water inside to clear a path. After a moment, they could no longer see him as he went deeper into the house in search of Julius. In that moment, Sylvia prayed a different prayer from the nights before. She prayed harder than she had ever prayed asking God to save her husband. She told Him he could take the house, even the gardens, but just please, spare her husband. Fedil finally emerged from the front door, black with smoke and heaving for air. Opal loosened her arms from Sylvia and ran to throw them around her own husband. It was then Sylvia realized he had come out alone, without Julius. The weakened body of her husband did not come out limped across the back of his only friend in the new town. Julius was still inside. At the mercy of the water brought in from every direction, what remained of the house were smoking windows and simmering embers. Fedil did not look at her, while Opal walked back over. Sylvia let her lifeless body slide to the ground before she reached her, still damp from the wash water.

It all happened so fast. One moment, she was soaking in the tub of water, the next, she was awake and her husband, her Junebug, was gone.

chapter 18

———◈———

SHE THOUGHT HIS DEATH WOULD make life easier. Somewhere deep inside something told her, and she believe it, that when she and Julius were no longer in this life together, she would be free. Sylvia would feel the freedom crawling on her skin like a caterpillar moments away from cocooning into the life of a butterfly. The very wings of the insect would be hers, to rise out of Mercy, or wherever, and fly. Hovering over the life left behind she would soar above and view the sights of a life now hers to enjoy as she pleased. No more achy bones from being beaten, since both the freedom and fantasy were now hers. With arms stretched towards the carefree living of the unknown, the imagined, even the make-believe, she would go, and she would go without worry.

The butterfly laid on the sill flat on its side, one wing set on top of the other in surrender. His body asleep...maybe even dead, like Julius.

Two weeks and four days had passed her through the window in the back room of Opal and Fedil's house. Counting the days and nights were her leisure. And the butterfly, it was all she had of any stir of freedom. In a painful way, Sylvia missed Julius. She missed the smell of a day's walk stirring from his sleeping body and the way he would jerk in slumber, fighting against the terrors of living a life awake. Some nights he would swing his arms and fists in his sleep, with such a force he was unable to use when he was awake. He struck at White folk's torture and Black folk's pain in his dreams. And at times, even her. Then, there were nights when the tears would steal away from the corners of his eyes, creeping creases and what Mistress called crow's feet stepping on his face. Even they were free...the tears. They knew where to go. They knew what to do with their freedom while Sylvia sat in a chair by a window, wrapped in a shawl, wondering.

"How about a walk to the store with me?" Opal remembered Sylvia was alive. Her words all the way to the store were mumbled chatter against her own thoughts.

Why did she not feel anything beyond the emptiness on her back, digging deeper into her spine? Why did she still think of the Julius' fists, swollen and cracked, bursting out of himself? Why did she not run from this place to a place where she could breathe and the air did not still carry the stench of burning wood and her salty tears?

When they left the store, headed back up the hill, Opal was still talking. It was not until she touched Sylvia's shoulder did any of her words sound recognizable. "Do you know him?"

"Who?" Sylvia asked, coming out of her mind chatter.

"The young man," Opal looked at her with a raised brow, both women huffing on the incline of the ground. "Outside the store."

"Probably not. Unless he's from Mercy, I don't know much of anyone outside of you, Livy and Fedil."

"With the way he stared at you, I figured you two must've known each other."

"I don't think so."

"Sylvia, you been here a while." She hinted at the amount of time Sylvia had been in Hartha Gables implying she should know more people, have done more things, and gone more places. Opal's life with Fedil was different from Sylvia and Julius'. She had the taste of both freedom and being loved on her tongue. Sylvia did not. She was not even familiar with the aroma. "Thought maybe you'd seen him around before."

"No." It was all she could say. She had not even noticed the man looking at her at the store.

That night, Sylvia did not have an appetite for Opal's dumplings or anything else. The comfort of her room and the company of her own thoughts were enough for her or at least she made herself believe it was. The room grew darker and Sylvia was no longer able to see the butterfly on the sill. What light the moon gave made a silhouette of everything against the wall behind the bed. She folded the shawl and placed it across the back of the chair. Sliding beneath the covers, she settled into the half of the bed belonging to her, leaving the other half for a man she missed in a peculiar way.

When morning came, the sunlight coming through the window warmed her closed eyelids. She was not ready to face another day she had no idea what to do with so she continued to lay there breathing calm and resisting morning. "Will you braid my hair today, Ma Syl?" She opened her eyes to sweet voice. Her darling eyes looked into Sylvia's as the child laid in the space left for Julius.

Propping her head on her hand, Sylvia smiled. "If that's what you want."

She braided her babygirl's hair, though it took longer than usual with her swollen hands and heavy soul. The time did not bother Alivia as she played with a carved horse Fedil had made her when they first arrived, back when they did not have a care in the world. Sylvia thought maybe she should not have had a care either, not now. For the first time in her life she was free, unbound by slavery or her husband's hand.

Her husband.

Her Julius.

She missed the man he was when he held her hand. He had been the only love in her life, even if the love was a wild ride of painful moments. Sylvia wondered if the thoughts of her dead husband were the same ones Mistress shared when Master Purvis died. The thought of writing a letter to Yuna back at Mercy crossed her mind. They deserved to know that Julius was gone. He had a mother, a sister, and a niece who loved him for his place in what was family, if nothing more. Her mind went back to Mistress as she tied the end of the braids into what resembled a bow. She was thankful for Opal and Fedil, but she had been living with them for a few weeks and was beginning to feel like a burden. Though each day, Opal reminded her she could stay with them for the rest of her life, if she wanted.

Sylvia did not know what to make of 'the rest of her life.' Like everyone, she did not know how much time she had left, but she knew what she had lived through was nothing to smile on. Other than her boys, her smiles were only for the herbs as they danced their way out of the ground. She craved the feel of soil in the creases of her hand. It was even the sticky goo of dough beneath her fingernails in the cookhouse she longed for.

She needed to go home.

When Sylvia broke the news to Fedil and Opal, as she expected, they were both saddened, but understood. The letter she mailed the next day was replied to in less than a month's time. Yuna spoke of being sad her uncle had died and how Ida had not reacted at all, as expected. Though Julius was her only son, they had long disconnected when the whip she held cut into his body. In the same breath, she spoke of how she was wearing thin running back and forth between the two plantations checking on Ida, teaching the children, and working for Mistress and Sister. She wrote about how her Mother had been through inevitable changes with Master Butler's return, yet did not go into detail about it. It was at the end of the letter she told her aunt of Mistress' plan to send for her in a few weeks. Sylvia had never felt more excited about anything in all her days.

A few mornings after the arrival of Yuna's letter, Opal invited her to take a walk into town to meet someone. Sylvia thought it was odd, especially when she did not take Alivia with them as they always did. The girl stayed behind, playing with the other children while Opal strapped the baby to her back and headed down the hill with Sylvia.

"I'm gone leave Creek here, if that's alright with you and Fedil." Sylvia told her as they walked.

"Oh, that would be wonderful! I'm sure Fedil gone be happy to hear that since he done took such a likin' to that horse. He is a beauty." Opal looked away with an expression not matching her words. Sylvia did not question it, assuming the emotions were getting the best of her, knowing her friend would be leaving soon.

They arrived at a house with two chairs on the porch. Before the two women could make their way up the few steps, a round and lively woman came out the front door wearing a big smile and giving out hugs. Constance, as she introduced herself to Sylvia, led them into her small home where she and her son, Tiny, a boy nearly as round as her but no older than ten years old, lived. It was later Opal told Sylvia Constance's husband was killed back in Mercy two days before emancipation arrived. He was caught by slave catchers when he returned from the North, having earned enough money to pay off the price his Master offered for his capture and buy his wife and son. Just outside of Mercy, they tortured him to his death, the reward for his capture not enough to rouse the slave catchers. Instead, they made an example of him, leaving his body at the entrance of his master's plantation, leaving Constance to break in half with grief. When word of freedom came days later, the first thing she did was pack up what little she and her son had, and headed away from the place where her man was killed. She went North, but ended up coming back to settle in Hartha Gables once it was established. She joked of being a southern women all the way down to her bones, the North not being the place for her.

"I just finish cooking a big pot of stew so plenty to eat and smack your lips at." Her voice was thunderous and demanded attention.

The house was tucked off the main road, but her window faced it, giving them something to concentrate on when she left to prepare iced tea.

"I'm sorry to hear 'bout your man." She said when she returned. "I know your heart in a million pieces. Can't tell you it ever mends, though. That's on you. You gotta make up your mind to live on or die with him." For a moment, Sylvia thought of Julius. What was left of his burnt body had been buried where her herb garden once was, the two things she loved in one place.

"Indeed." Sylvia sipped the tea, holding onto its mint aroma. Without realizing it, she had closed her eyes and drifted away. To her gardens, the burned ones and the one she longed for back in Mercy. She opened her eyes to Constance's own, big and round like the rest of her. "I'm sorry. I'm just wrapping my head 'round everything going on."

"Nothing wrong with that." Opal patted the back of Sylvia's hand as she shifted the baby from one knee to the other.

"I know it's a lot. Plenty to get through. But you will." Constance shifted on her chair. Her hips hung across the sides of the seat, though, she somehow looked comfortable in what she called her own. "How ya know my sister?" Her head tilted towards Opal.

"Julius knew Fedil. I raise Livy when he and Opal came here."

"Right, right."

Opal gave Constance a sideways look, then a nod. Their unspoken conversation was brief, but understood between only the two of them.

"Yes. We Julius and Sylvia. Well," the reality settled in. "Well, I'm Sylvia. From Mercy."

"Yes you are. You the one take care of the niece for 'em to get here safe." Constance turned the glass to her head then directed her conversation to Opal. "These the ones," asking and answering herself.

Sylvia was confused. "I don't know what you mean? You say the niece? Livy like my daughter, but I just met Opal when we got here. We close now, but I never know'd her in a sister way."

"That ain't what I'm talking bout. I'm talking about Livy momma."

"Livy momma?" Sylvia was even more confused. "You mean Opal?"

"Opal? Well sure 'nough Opal like momma to her cause she raise her up this far. But neither one of you spit the child out. Her God-given momma done that."

"Constance, wait. I don't get a bit of what you're saying. What're you talking about? Opal , you ain't my Livy's momma?"

"Sylvia, that's what I wanted to tell you. Alivia is your kin, not mine. Julius blood."

"How so?" Her mind ran around in all kinds of confusion. "Wait. You mean to tell me, Julius know'd babygirl was his kin? His niece?"

"Yeah, he knew." Opal said putting the baby on her shoulder and patting his back. "He knew and that's why he was fine with taking her for a while. That and...and well he told Fedil when he bought Alivia to you about how much you miss your boys and never got to keep any of your own children."

Part of Sylvia felt betrayed, the other part of her whirled in wonder. "So if you ain't her momma, who is?"

"Opal raised that baby since she was born. Loved her with everything in her, but it ain't her womb she come from."

"Well who womb then?"

"Her own momma. Your husband sister."

"My husband sister?" Sylvia gasped. "Nella Jo?"

"I don't know what her name is. I just know Fedil bring the baby home one day and me and Opal looking at each other sideways trying to figure out where it come from. He say the momma tried to get rid of it, sent it up the river buried in a basket. Don't know why, but he saw what he saw. He hid. He saw her when she pushed it out in the water and walked away like it was dead to her. Short while after, he heard the crying and swam out to get the basket and brought her home."

"You lying to me!" Sylvia did not really mean the words that fell from her mouth, but it's what came out in her state of shock. Her mouth hung open, waiting for Constance to change her story.

"I'm telling you the truth. Opal, tell her." Constance shifted in her chair again. "She love that child like her own and when she had to send her to y'all to make sure the child 'scape death one more time 'til they make it safe and sound here, it tore her up. Only thing make that child not hers is blood in they veins."

"Does Livy know?"

"No. Ain't nobody tell her." Opal said. "Everybody deserve to know they own truths. Just been waiting for the right time to tell her. I think now that time, with you getting ready to leave and all. As much as I love her, Sylvia she deserve to be with her family." She paused and looked into Sylvia's eyes. "And you deserve her. She love you.."

Constance jumped back in, interrupting. "How you not know? Who you think you been raising all this time?"

Sylvia was embarrassed to say she did not have the courage to ask questions. She thought maybe she was a child of Julius's and he did not have the heart to tell her. She had a head full of explanations of why she had kept Alivia like she was her own but none of them were ever confirmed.

"Well, you know now, and that's what matter. Now what you wanna do with that knowing is on you."

Sylvia nodded as she thought about Nella Jo and tried to imagine what would ever make her do such a thing.

"We gotta go." She said standing from the chair and handing Constance the half drank cup of tea. "Come on Opal. I need to see my Livy."

Mistress sent for Sylvia on a Thursday morning. Little did she know, the original plan was to have the driver come for her the following weekend, but Ida was ill.

Sylvia stepped from the wagon with a shawl around her shoulders warding off the bite of autumn turning to winter. If only Ida could see her from the window where she watched the world go on, she would have something to say about the new dress Mistress had sent. She would probably tell her whatever she put in that tea, knocking that white man over must have been real good for his wife to still be thanking her. The thought and the slight smile of hearing Ida's voice in her head both left when she walked through the open door of the cabin. Ida's face was lifeless as she leaned from the side of her pallet vomiting into a pail. She heaved and let her weak body fall back onto the pallet, mouth still open, begging for air.

Yuna was at her side, wiping at her mouth and forehead. Sylvia stood in the doorway, too sad to move. The woman who had been like a mother to her since she had married her son was dying, weeks after her only son.

"You ain't gotta stand over there like I'm already dead and stinkin'." Ida pushed the words out. "Get on over here. Yuna, move that pail."

"Ms. Ida, I'm sorry…"

"For what?" She interrupted. "You the one call death here to get me?"

"Oh no. That's not what I mean."

"Well that's too bad, 'cause I was gonna thank you. Too old to still be stuck here waiting to die." Sylvia wanted to smile, but it wasn't until she finally met Ida's eyes, trying for a slight smile of her own, she gave in.

"You know I love you."

"Ain't never thought different." Ida tried to turn onto her side. "Question is do you know the same thing."

"Sure I do." She swallowed the tears crawling up her throat. "You been like a mother to me…"

"Enough of all that." Ida shooed her hand at Sylvia's words. "This life give us what we need in the people we need it in. You got that White lady over there been just as good to you in her own way as I been. Don't make no never mind 'bout being like mother, sister, whatever. Just be thankful." She was finally settled on her side and Yuna slid behind her and rubbed her back.

"You need to be resting."

"And you need to be asking for forgiveness of all the foolishness you done done in this world, but that ain't happening right now either, is it?" Ida said to the corner of the room. "Now hush up."

Sylvia had not even noticed Nella Jo sitting on Ida's only chair in the dark corner. She looked different since the last time Sylvia had seen her, but this wasn't the time to try to figure out how.

"Ma'am," the driver's voice called from outside. "I'll be leaving now. Your things will be over at the Purvis house as instructed."

"Thank you kindly," Sylvia said through the door then turned back to Ida, this time coming closer. The shawl fell to the floor as she knelt on the floor beside her. Yuna moved the pail around a bit more. She flashed a smile at her aunt, in place of the hug they both would exchange later, when the time was right. For the first time, Sylvia realized how much her Livy's smile favored Yuna's.

Ida's hair was silver with not a single strand of black anywhere in the long mane draped over her shoulders and rolled onto her back beneath Yuna's touch.

"Where's that babygirl of mine?"

The question made Sylvia look over at Nella Jo, sitting in the chair, making a mess of some embroidery. Turning back to Ida, "Alivia is doing very well. I'll bring her to see you soon." Again, she looked over at Nella Jo. "She's a wonderful little girl, doing just fine. Regardless of how things started out for her."

"Huh?" Yuna perked up to the words with curiosity.

"Don't worry about it, child. Everything don't need to be known." Ida looked right at Sylvia when she said the words at Yuna, her eyes, half closed. "Everything known did not have to be told. Sometimes, a secret the best thing you can hold onto."

When darkness fell over Mercy the night Sylvia came home, she had never felt more free in all her life.

all my love

...goes out to you, to surround and embrace you with my most humble bow of gratitude.

...to my Love, Tonya, my Sun, Jaiden, and my Source, M. Boles.

...to my editorial team: Lenore Simon, Nelly Rosario, Lula Baker, and Aziza Aremo.

...to my V.I.B.E. (Voice In Between Ethers), Lynn D. of Heaven's Whispers.

...to the Queens of ebonyLotus WriteLife Sessions and the Kings and Queens of Black Writers with Purpose.

...to the staff and tour guides of Laura Plantation (Vacherie, LA) and Ashtabula Plantation (Pendleton, SC)

...to my writing partners: Fiona Z., Kimberly P.S, Leteisha R., Jameelah R., and Maliika W., and my historical researcher, Robin M.

...to my fabulous assistants: D.M. and Michelle W., my BetaBoo: Be A., and my management and publishing team.

...and to all of you, named and unnamed here...
...from all of me...

...thank you.

about the author

Brook Blander is the author and poet of six literary works, including her most recent historical/women's fiction novel *The Secrets of Mercy* (2013).

Her short fiction and poetry has appeared in numerous anthologies including Michigan's Thursday Night Write, Detour Memphis, and G.R.I.T.S. (Girls Raised In The South) under her pseudonym, B.B. Doyle.

Blander is a member of the Historical Novel Society and the International Association of Journal Writers.

A southerner at heart, Blander is a native of Savannah, GA now residing in North Texas where she is an editor, publisher, and writing coach at ebonyLotus WriteLife™ Studio. She flows in the joy of her life as a mother, partner, sister, auntie and goddess-mommy. She lives in the blessings of her ancestors who guide and inspire her daily.